THE GAME'S AFOOT!

Now, match wits with the world's greatest consulting detective. And have no fear — if you don't completely succeed at first, just play again! It might be wise to keep in mind Holmes' advice to Watson and all would-be detectives:

"It is an old maxim of mine," he said, "that when you have eliminated the impossible, whatever remains, however improbable, must be the truth."

SHERLOCK HOLMES SOLO MYSTERIES™ — developed by Iron Crown Enterprises — present a series of living mystery novels designed for solitary game play. In each gamebook, the reader is the detective who must solve or prevent a crime — with Sherlock Holmes and Dr. Watson as allies.

Look for a new gamebook in the SHERLOCK HOLMES SOLO MYSTERIES™ series every other month from Berkley and Iron Crown Enterprises!

D0878291

System Editor: S. Coleman Charlton

Production: Kurt Fischer, Richard H. Britton, Coleman Charlton, Jessica Ney, John Ruemmler, Suzanne Young

Cover Graphics: Richard H. Britton

THE CROWN VS DR. WATSON

by Gerald Lientz

Content Editor: John David Ruemmler
Managing Editor: Kevin Barrett
Cover Art : Daniel Horne
Illustrations by: Bob Versandi

BERKLEY BOOKS, NEW YORK

CHARACTER RECORD

Name: DAVID PHILLIPS

Skill	Bonus	Equipment:
Athletics	+1	1) POCKET KNIFE
Artifice	+1	2) PENCIL
Observation	+1	3) NOTEBOOK
Intuition	+1	4)
Communication	+1	5)
Scholarship	+1	6)
		7)

Money:		
_____ pence		8)
_30_ shillings		9)
_____ guineas		10)
_4_ pounds		11)

NOTES:

CHARACTER RECORD

Name:

Skill	Bonus	Equipment:
Athletics	_____	1)
Artifice	_____	2)
Observation	_____	3)
Intuition	_____	4)
Communication	_____	5)
Scholarship	_____	6)
		7)

Money: _____pence   8)
       _____shillings   9)
       _____guineas   10)
       _____pounds   11)

NOTES:

CHARACTER RECORD

Name:

Skill	Bonus	Equipment:
Athletics	_____	1)
Artifice	_____	2)
Observation	_____	3)
Intuition	_____	4)
Communication	_____	5)
Scholarship	_____	6)
		7)

Money: _____pence — 8)

_____shillings — 9)

_____guineas — 10)

_____pounds — 11)

NOTES:

CLUE SHEET

- ☐ **A** _____
- ☐ **B** _____
- ☐ **C** _____
- ☐ **D** _____
- ☐ **E** _____
- ☐ **F** _____
- ☐ **G** _____
- ☐ **H** _____
- ☐ **I** _____
- ☐ **J** _____
- ☐ **K** _____
- ☐ **L** _____
- ☐ **M** _____
- ☐ **N** _____
- ☐ **O** _____
- ☐ **P** _____
- ☐ **Q** _____
- ☐ **R** _____
- ☐ **S** _____
- ☐ **T** _____
- ☐ **U** _____
- ☐ **V** _____
- ☐ **W** _____
- ☐ **X** _____
- ☐ **Y** _____
- ☐ **Z** _____

DECISIONS & DEDUCTIONS SHEET

- ☐ 1 _____
- ☐ 2 _____
- ☐ 3 _____
- ☐ 4 _____
- ☐ 5 _____
- ☐ 6 _____
- ☐ 7 _____
- ☐ 8 _____
- ☐ 9 _____
- ☐ 10 _____
- ☐ 11 _____
- ☐ 12 _____
- ☐ 13 _____
- ☐ 14 _____
- ☐ 15 _____
- ☐ 16 _____
- ☐ 17 _____

DECISIONS & DEDUCTIONS
SHEET

☐ 18 _____

☐ 19 _____

☐ 20 _____

☐ 21 _____

☐ 22 _____

☐ 23 _____

☐ 24 _____

☐ 25 _____

☐ 26 _____

☐ 27 _____

☐ 28 _____

☐ 29 _____

_____

_____

_____

_____

_____

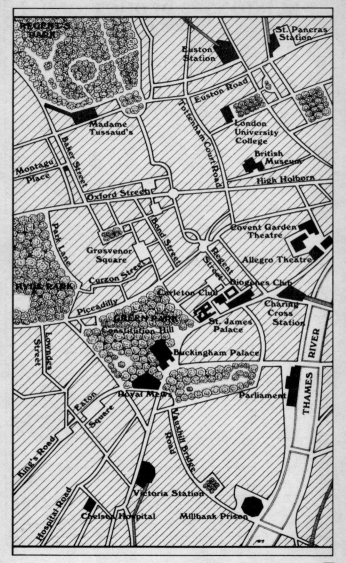

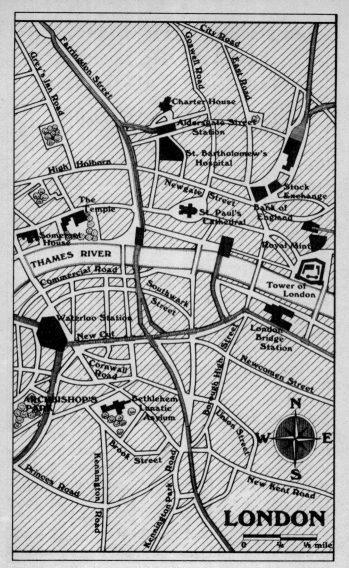

AN INTRODUCTION TO THE WORLD OF SHERLOCK HOLMES

HOLMES AND WATSON

First appearing in "A Study in Scarlet" in Beeton's Christmas Annual of 1887, Sherlock Holmes remains a remarkably vigorous and fascinating figure for a man of such advanced years. The detective's home and office at 221B Baker Street are shrines now, not simply rooms in which Holmes slept and deduced and fiddled with the violin when he could not quite discern the significance of a clue or put his finger on a criminal's twisted motive.

We know both a great deal and very little about Sherlock Holmes as a person. The son of a country squire (and grandson of the French artist Vernet's sister), Holmes seems to have drawn little attention to himself until his University days, where his extraordinary talents for applying logic, observation and deduction to solving petty mysteries earned him a reputation as something of a genius. Taking the next logical step, Holmes set up a private consulting detective service, probably in 1878. Four years later, he met and formed a partnership with a former military surgeon, Dr. John Watson. Four novels and fifty-six short stories tell us everything we know of the odd pair and their extraordinary adventures.

Less a well-rounded individual than a collection of contradictory and unusual traits, Holmes seldom exercised yet was a powerful man of exceptional speed of foot. He would eagerly work for days on a case with no rest and little food, yet in periods of idleness would refuse to get out of bed for days. Perhaps his most telling comment appears in "The Adventure of the Mazarin Stone:"

I am a brain, Watson. The rest of me is a mere appendix.

Holmes cared little for abstract knowledge, once noting that it mattered not to him if the earth circled the sun or vice versa. Yet he could identify scores of types of tobacco ash or perfume by sight and odor, respectively. Criminals and their modus operandi obsessed him; he pored over London's sensational newspapers religiously.

A master of disguise, the detective successfully presented himself as an aged Italian priest, a drunken groom, and even an old woman! A flabbergasted Watson is the perfect foil to Holmes, who seems to take special delight in astonishing his stuffy if kind cohort.

In "The Sign of Four," Holmes briefly noted the qualities any good detective should possess in abundance (if possible, intuitively): heightened powers of observation and deduction, and a broad range of precise (and often unusual) knowledge. In this *Sherlock Holmes Solo Mysteries*™ adventure, you will have ample opportunity to test yourself in these areas, and through replaying the adventure, to improve your detective skills.

Although impressive in talent and dedication to his profession, Sherlock Holmes was by no means perfect. Outfoxed by Irene Adler, Holmes readily acknowledged defeat by "the woman" in "A Scandal in Bohemia." In 1887, he admitted to Watson that three men had outwitted him (and Scotland Yard). The lesson Holmes himself drew from these failures was illuminating:

> *Perhaps when a man has special knowledge and special powers like my own, it rather encourages him to seek a complex explanation when a simpler one is at hand.*

So learn to trust your own observations and deductions — when they make sense and match the physical evidence and the testimony of trusted individuals — don't rush to judgment, and if you like and the adventure allows, consult Holmes or Watson for advice and assistance.

VICTORIAN LONDON

When Holmes lived and worked in London, from the early 1880's until 1903, the Victorian Age was much more than a subject of study and amusement. Queen Victoria reigned over England for more than 60 years, an unheard of term of rule; her tastes and inhibitions mirrored and formed those of English society. Following the Industrial Revolution of roughly 1750-1850, England leaped and stumbled her way from a largely pastoral state into a powerful, flawed factory of a nation. (The novels of Charles Dickens dramatically depict this cruel, exhilarating period of sudden social change.) Abroad, imperialism planted the Union Jack (and implanted English mores) in Africa, India, and the Far East, including Afghanistan, where Dr. Watson served and was wounded.

Cosmopolitan and yet reserved, London in the late Nineteenth Century sported over six million inhabitants, many from all over the world; it boasted the high society of Park Lane yet harbored a seedy Chinatown where opium could be purchased and consumed like tea. To orient yourself, consult the two-page map of London on pages 10 and 11. You will see that Baker Street is located just south of Regent's Park, near the Zoological Gardens, in the heart of the stylish West End of the city. Railway and horse-drawn carriages were the preferred means of transport; people often walked, and thieves frequently ran to get from one place to another.

THE GAME'S AFOOT!

Now, match wits with the world's greatest consulting detective. And have no fear — if you don't completely succeed at first, just play again! It might be wise to keep in mind Holmes' advice to Watson and all would-be detectives:

"It is an old maxim of mine," he said, "that when you have eliminated the impossible, whatever remains, however improbable, must be the truth."

Good luck and good hunting!

THE SHERLOCK HOLMES SOLO MYSTERIES™ GAME SYSTEM

THE GAMEBOOK

This gamebook describes hazards, situations, and locations that may be encountered during your adventures. As you read the text sections, you will be given choices as to what actions you may take. What text section you read will depend on the directions in the text and whether the actions you attempt succeed or fail.

Text sections are labeled with three-digit numbers (e.g.,"365"). Read each text section only when told to do so by the text.

PICKING A NUMBER

Many times during your adventures in this game-book you will need to pick a number (between 2 and 12). There are several ways to do this:

1) Turn to the Random Number Table at the end of this book, use a pencil (or pen or similar object), close your eyes, and touch the Random Number Table with the pencil. The number touched is the number which you have picked. If your pencil falls on a line, just repeat the process. **or**

2) Flip to a random page in the book and look at the small boxed number in the inside, bottom corner of the page. This number is the number which you have picked. **or**

3) If you have two six-sided dice, roll them. The result is the number which you have picked. (You can also roll one six-sided die twice and add the results.)

Often you will be instructed to pick a number and add a "bonus". When this happens, treat results of more than 12 as "12" and treat results of less than 2 as "2".

3

INFORMATION, CLUES, AND SOLVING THE MYSTERY

During play you will discover certain clues (e.g., a footprint, murder weapon, a newspaper article) and make certain decisions and deductions (e.g., you decide to follow someone, you deduce that the butler did it). Often the text will instruct you to do one of the following:

Check Clue xx or *Check Decision xx* or *Check Deduction xx.*

"xx" is a letter for Clues and a number for Decisions and Deductions. When this occurs, check the appropriate box on the "Clue Record Sheets" found at the beginning of the book. You should also record the information gained and note the text section number on the line next to the box. You may copy or photocopy these sheets for your own use.

Other useful information not requiring a "check" will also be included in the text. You may want to take other notes, so a "NOTES" space is provided at the bottom of your "Character Record". Remember that some of the clues and information given may be meaningless or unimportant (i.e., red herrings).

EQUIPMENT AND MONEY

Whenever you acquire money and equipment, record them on your Character Record in the spaces provided. Pennies (1 Pence), shillings (12 pence), guineas (21 shillings), and pounds (20 shillings) are "money" and may be used during your adventures to pay for food, lodging, transport, bribes, etc. Certain equipment may affect your abilities as indicated by the text.

You begin the adventure with the money noted on the completed Character Record sheet near the front of the book.

CHOOSING A CHARACTER

There are two ways to choose a character:

1) You can use the completely created character provided at the beginning of the book. **or**

2) You can create your own character using the simple character development system included in the next section of this book.

STARTING TO PLAY

After reading the rules above and choosing a character to play, start your adventures by reading the Prologue found after the rules section. From this point on, read the passages as indicated by the text.

CREATING YOUR OWN CHARACTER

If you do not want to create your own character, use the pre-created character found in the front of this book. If you decide to create your own character, follow the directions given in this section. Keep track of your character on the blank Character Record found in the front of this book. It is advisable to enter information in pencil so that it can be erased and updated. If necessary, you may copy or photocopy this Character Record for your own use.

As you go through this character creation process, refer to the pre-created character in the front of the book as an example.

SKILLS

The following 6 "Skill Areas" affect your chances of accomplishing certain actions during your adventures.

1) **Athletics** (includes fitness, adroitness, fortitude, pugnacity, fisticuffs): This skill reflects your ability to perform actions and maneuvers requiring balance, coordination, speed, agility, and quickness. Such actions can include fighting, avoiding attacks, running, climbing, riding, swimming, etc.

2) **Artifice** (includes trickery, disguise, stealth, eavesdropping): Use this skill when trying to move without being seen or heard (i.e., sneaking), trying to steal something, picking a lock, escaping from bonds, disguising yourself, and many other similar activities.

3) **Intuition** (includes sensibility, insight, reasoning, deduction, luck): This skill reflects your ability to understand and correlate information, clues, etc. It also reflects your ability to make guesses and to have hunches.

4) **Communication** (includes interviewing, acting, mingling, negotiating, diplomacy): This skill reflects your ability to talk with, negotiate with, and gain information from people. It also reflects your "social graces" and social adaptivity, as well as your ability to act and to hide your own thoughts and feelings.

5) **Observation** (includes perception, alertness, empathy): This skill reflects how much information you gather through visual perception.

6) **Scholarship** (includes education, science, current events, languages): This skill reflects your training and aptitude with various studies and sciences: foreign languages, art, history, current events, chemistry, tobaccory, biology, etc.

SKILL BONUSES

For each of these skills, you will have a Skill Bonus that is used when you attempt certain actions. When the text instructs you to "add your bonus," it is referring to these Skill Bonuses. Keep in mind that these "bonuses" can be negative as well as positive.

When you start your character, you have six "+1 bonuses" to assign to your skills.

You may assign more than one "+1 bonuses" to a given skill, but no more than three to any one skill. Thus, two "+1 bonuses" assigned to a skill will be a "+2 bonus", and three "+1 bonuses" will be a "+3 bonus". Each of these bonuses should be recorded in the space next to the appropriate skill on your Character Record.

If you do not assign any "+1 bonuses" to a skill, you must record a "-2 bonus" in that space.

During play you may acquire equipment or injuries that may affect your bonuses. Record these modifications in the "Bonus" spaces.

Bobby Chambers: Servant at the "Three Continents" Club.

Lord Grayson: Son of the Earl of Waynesborough, Member of the "Three Continents."

Sir George Grant: Member of the "Three Continents."

Mycroft Holmes: Brother of the late Sherlock Holmes.

John Howard: Member of the "Three Continents."

Lord Howard: Member of the "Three Continents."

Edwin Johnson: Butler at the "Three Continents."

Captain Edward Lawrence: Army officer, member of the "Three Continents."

Alexander Lewis: Member of the "Three Continents."

Captain Sherwood Locke: Provost Officer, friend of Mycroft Holmes.

Thomas Martin: Member of the "Three Continents."

Christopher Marshall: Friend of Dr. Watson, member of the "Three Continents."

Inspector Alec McDonald: Scotland Yard officer assigned to the investigation.

Sir Terrence Milton, Baronet: Businessman, member of the "Three Continents"; murder victim.

Miss Ellen Phipps: Friend of Dr. Watson.

John Strickland: Chairman of the "Three Continents."

Thomas Sullivan: Member of the "Three Continents."

John Symington: London businessman.

Earl of Waynesborough: Member of the "Three Continents."

AN INTRODUCTORY NOTE

In this case the player-detective is a former Baker Street Irregular, who, inspired by Sherlock Holmes, acquired enough education to become a detective in a small way himself.

The case is set in early 1894. Two and a half years ago, the player read the shocking news of Sherlock Holmes' death in an accident in Switzerland, news confirmed recently when Dr. Watson published the story, "The Final Problem," which described the circumstances of Holmes' death. Though aware of his own inferior skills, the player tries to fight crime in London in the tradition of his great mentor.

You have a pocketknife, a notebook, a pencil, and thirty shillings and four pounds in cash. You may now begin your investigation. Enter these items on your Character Record. Good luck. The game is afoot.

PROLOGUE

Roaming London one brisk winter morning, you decide to stop at the store operated by Wiggins, former chief of the Baker Street Irregulars, and read the morning papers. Your old leader and friend greets you cheerfully, then points to a story headlined on several papers. At his urging you read several accounts of a murder in "The Three Continents Club." You see that Sir Terrence Milton, a noted businessman with "interests in many corners of the empire," was the victim. While no arrest has been made, Inspector Alec McDonald of Scotland Yard reports that, "The police are pursuing their inquiries carefully, and an arrest can be expected shortly, as soon as the police have verified all aspects of the case."

You sigh a little. "They would probably have the killer behind bars now, Wiggins," you say, "if Mr. Holmes was still with us in London."

"Perhaps," he answers, "and perhaps not. One of my mates on the force stopped by and told me something of the case. He said the evidence points like a knife straight at Dr. Watson, Mr. Holmes' old friend. In a case like that Mr. Holmes might not have wanted to find the proof to send his best mate for a date with Jack Ketch."

"Dr. Watson!" you say in astonishment. "How could anyone suspect him of committing a crime? He's a well-known writer and a successful doctor."

"My mate says the evidence was so convincing that he would have been arrested by now, except that Inspector McDonald refused to do it. He worked with both Mr. Holmes and Dr. Watson, you know." After talking for a few more minutes you return to your lodgings. There, you are amazed to find a note from Mycroft Holmes, brother of the late detective, asking you to visit him at his rooms in Pall Mall. Naturally, you hurry out to answer this summons.

Mycroft himself admits you to his rooms. He is a large, heavily built man. In spite of being much heavier, you can see a strong resemblance between him and his late brother Sherlock. He thanks you for your prompt response, and explains that renovations in his offices have made it necessary for him to take a few days away from his work for the government. He then introduces you to his other guest, Inspector Alec McDonald of Scotland Yard.

"So you want me to look into the Milton murder," you say boldly, hoping to make an impression on the men.

"You may be right, Mr. Holmes," McDonald laughs. "The young man's technique puts me in mind of your brother."

"It was hardly a brilliant deduction," Mycroft answers, "as every newspaper in the city reported that you were the officer in charge of the investigation."

"But why did you want me?" you ask. "If I read the papers correctly, you expect to make an arrest shortly."

"I do, lad, and more's the pity," McDonald answers. "I've looked into the matter as carefully as I can, and all the evidence ties a rope around one neck—and there's the rub."

"Mr. McDonald believes that the evidence points to Dr. John Watson, Sherlock's old friend and comrade," Mycroft interrupts. "I find it difficult to believe he would commit murder, and for the sake of my brother I want the case investigated by an independent pair of eyes. If poor Sherlock were still with us, I'm sure he'd clear the doctor soon enough."

"That may be so," McDonald laughs, "and I wish Mr. Holmes were still in London, for while he showed us our foolishness often enough, he also seized many a scoudrel. But if you are interested in investigating this matter," he adds, turning to you, "I will give you an outline of the evidence."

"Certainly, sir," you answer. "I understand the killing occurred in 'The Three Continents Club?'"

"Aye, that it did, not two blocks from where we're sitting," the Inspector answers. "There were not many men in the club last night, only a few kept in the city by business. Four of them, Sir Terrence Milton, Dr. Watson, Mr. Christopher Marshall and Mr. Thomas Martin, spent the hours after supper in a game of whist. When Dr. Watson and Mr. Marshall won the decisive rubber with a slam in the last hand, Sir Terrence accused Dr. Watson of cheating, saying he must have learned the finer arts of card playing in his days in the wilds of America and Australia.

"Well, Dr. Watson is no man to take such a suggestion, as you may know, and he shouted at Sir Terrence, accusing him of cheating many a man through his crooked companies. I understand that Dr. Watson lost a considerable sum when Sir Terrence's latest company, the Ivory Coast Mining Venture, failed. The police have been looking closely into that company, since its fall.

"Well, Sir Terrence answered by suggesting that if Dr. Watson had spent less time showing a certain singer the sights of London and more studying the prospectus, he wouldn't have mistaken a high-risk venture for a safe and sound investment—but that was all he said," the Inspector concludes," for Dr. Watson put his fist between Sir Terrence's eyes at this point and stretched him on the carpet."

"What's that about a woman?" Mycroft asks. "You didn't mention that before."

"I'm sorry, sir, I must have forgotten," McDonald answers. "According to his friend Marshall, Watson has been seeing quite a lot of one of the singers performing at Prism Hall in Piccadilly. Nothing wrong with that, of course. The doctor's wife died more than a year ago."

Mycroft nods heavily. "Sherlock always said that Watson had the expertise where women were concerned. And it's gotten him properly into trouble this time." He thinks a moment and turns to you. "You must investigate the scene of the crime and interview the witnesses. I have a friend, Captain Locke of the Provost's Office, who is very familiar with the night life of London. I will ask him to investigate this woman. But go on, Inspector McDonald; continue your description of events at the club."

"Thank you. Well, the other members broke up the fight, and a little before nine o'clock Sir Terrence went upstairs. Watson went up a little later and sat in a billiard room to have a drink and settle his temper, or so he says. He left the room about nine-thirty, and a servant went in immediately to fetch the empty glass and tidy things. The servant found Sir Terrence lying in the corner with his head smashed in. He says no one else could have entered the room after Watson left. He ran screaming into the hall, the other members rushed in, and they summoned us. The case looks very clear-cut to me. Watson was the only man in the room, he had just argued with Milton, and he had other reasons to hate Milton, as his bogus company cost the Doctor a good deal of his investment capital. According to Marshall and others, Watson has been having a hard go of it lately, between the death of Mr. Holmes and his wife, and all sorts of financial problems. His medical practice suffered badly while his wife was sick. He has lost his outside income as he can no longer write about Mr. Holmes."

"Was the weapon Dr. Watson's?" you ask.

"No, anyone in the room could have used it," McDonald answers. "The killer used the poker from the fireplace. The fire had burned low, and it's a little surprising that Watson didn't look for the poker to stir it up. But less surprising if he had just used the poker to kill a man!"

"And what does Dr. Watson say he was doing in the room for the half hour he was there?"

"He says he just sat by the fire, drank his brandy and read a newspaper," McDonald answers. "He claims that he was shocked to realize that there was a dead man in the corner for the entire period of time."

You nod, trying to think of holes in this argument.

- *If you ask McDonald more questions*, **turn to 159.**
- *Otherwise*, **turn to 443.**

100

You race after the man, running as fast as you can, trying to keep the villain in sight. *Check Decision 1.* **Pick a number** *and add your Athletics bonus:*

- *If 2-6,* **turn to 113.**
- *If 7-12,* **turn to 208.**

101

You pause for a moment, pondering further questions you might ask Captain Lawrence. Does this officer hold the key to unlocking the investigation? Should you ask him further questions?

- *If you ask what he did when he heard of the murder,* **turn to 335.**
- *If you are through with Lawrence,* **turn to 436.**
- *Otherwise,* **turn to 116.**

102

You wonder if Lewis knew anything about the trapdoor in the billiard room.

- *If you ask him,* **turn to 197.**
- *Otherwise,* **turn to 311.**

103

You take a hansom to the building where Symington has his offices, get off half a block away, and walk towards the building. Can the businessman help you solve the case?

- *If you checked Decision 9,* **turn to 363.**
- *Otherwise,* **turn to 477.**

104

"When you were in the room, did you notice that one of the little tables was knocked over?" you ask. "The one by the chair nearest the windows."

"No, sir, I'm afraid I didn't notice," he answers. "I had eyes for nothing but the body, sir, until Mr. Strickland sent us running errands and preparing for the arrival of the police." **Turn to 181.**

105

As you listen outside Symington's door, a gun discharges. You hear a series of thumps inside the room. Knowing you can do nothing for Symington now, you hide at the end of the hall and watch. Marshall hurries out and races down the steps. You go into the office and find Symington lying dead, a bust of Wellington smashed across the back of his head. You have no doubt that Marshall used the bust to hide the damage done by his gun. *Check Clue T.* **Turn to 546.**

106

"Yes, I know who it was," you answer, reaching back to touch the sore spot. "It was Marshall. He visited Symington, and I followed him when he left. He obviously got the better of me."

"Well," the Inspector answers grimly, "it shall be the rope for Mr. Marshall then. When I heard what happened to you,

I went to see Symington myself. He was dead, shot through the head. I shall get some men and see if I can bring Marshall to justice. You rest yourself, and let your poor head heal up. That was a brutal blow you took." As the police detective leaves, you lie back and try to relax. While you haven't failed completely in this investigation, you certainly haven't succeeded.

• *If you begin the case again,* **turn to the Prologue.**
• *If you would like the case explained,* **turn to 435.**

107

A few necessary errands fill the rest of the morning. At noon you stop at your lodgings to check your mail. Amid the bills and personal letters there is a note from Mycroft Holmes, asking you to visit him at home immediately. You wonder whether he has made some crucial discovery in the case and hurry to his lodgings to see him.

Mycroft greets you with his customary politeness. "Thank you for coming promptly," he says, leading you into a small study. "Captain Locke succeeded in his investigations of the lady's background, and I thought you would like to hear his report."

As you nod in agreement, another man enters the room, dressed in a uniform trimmed in the fashion of the provost department. He is a tall lean man, with bushy, greying sideburns, a thick mustache and heavy eyebrows. The tinted glasses that hide his eyes are almost hidden among all the hair.

"This is Captain Locke," Mycroft announces. "The army very kindly loaned his services to me, and he has carried out his part of the case very quickly indeed."

"What did you find out about the lady?" you ask.

Locke consults some notes and begins to speak in a soft, almost toneless voice. "The lady is a singer named Miss Ellen Phipps, who is now performing at the Prism Hall. Everyone who knows her speaks well of her. She is engaged to be married as soon as she completes her current series of performances. Her relations with Watson were of the most innocent kind."

"They were?" you ask in surprise. "Some of the men who talked about it believed that the Doctor was likely to marry her."

"There is no evidence of that," Locke answers. "If you review the evidence carefully, you will trace all those stories to one source. Probably you will find some friend of Watson's who saw them together and jumped to conclusions. Given Watson's affinity for the fairer sex, it was an understandable mistake."

"But what's the true story?" you demand.

"Miss Phipps is an old school friend of the late Mrs. Watson," Locke tells you, again consulting his notes. "She came to see her friend and found to her distress that she had died. Watson, gentleman that he is, naturally invited his visitor out to supper. A few days later Watson went to hear her sing. A drunk in the audience accosted the lady, and Watson came to her defense. He saw her home safely, and that was the last time he talked with her. You can rest assured that the lady had nothing to do with the murder." *Check Deduction 25.*

- *If you checked Clue U,* **turn to 498.**
- *Otherwise,* **turn to 244.**

108

Remembering that Marshall left Symington's office only a few minutes ago, you find it impossible to believe Symington's death was an accident. You bend over the body, move the bust and carefully examine Symington's head. As you suspected, you find a bullet wound. You have no doubt regarding who killed Symington and send for McDonald. He arrives with several constables, listens to your story, and nods in agreement. "It must be Marshall!" he agrees. With McDonald and the constables, you hurry to Marshall's house, hoping that he has not fled the city. *Check Deduction 21.* **Turn to 338.**

109

Before the captain begins his explanation, you wonder how this man solved such a complicated case so quickly. You stare intently at the Captain as he starts to speak. **Pick a number** *and add your Observation bonus:*

- *If 2-7,* **turn to 382.**
- *If 8-12,* **turn to 532.**

110

Symington waits almost a minute to answer, then begins to chuckle. "A hidden partner, you say. It is amazing how every businessman is supposed to have some hidden partner who is responsible for his success. They have even said the same thing about me. They never want to admit that any particular man has any ability; they would rather credit some mysterious mastermind." He laughs again. **Turn to 438.**

111

Locke listens to your explanation, then nods. "At least you have no definite proof that Marshall was anywhere else, and he is the only one without an alibi. That will do." **Turn to 318.**

112

You wonder whether Marshall knows anything of use and try to think of the proper questions to get this information.

- *If you ask him what he did until the body was discovered,* **turn to 402.**
- *If you are finished questioning him,* **turn to 405.**
- *Otherwise,* **turn to 308.**

113

Marshall proves to be faster than you are and also knows the streets around here very well. After he turns one corner, he vanishes by the time you round it. Desperately, you look for traces of his passage. **Pick a number** *and add your Observation bonus:*

- *If 2-6,* **turn to 114.**
- *If 7-12,* **turn to 119.**

114

You cannot locate Marshall anywhere. The police join you, and by diligent searching and questioning you eventually learn that Marshall took a steam launch down the river. McDonald gives orders for the constables to return to Scotland Yard and to take the steps necessary to catch Marshall before he can leave the country.

"Mr. Holmes will not like our report," he comments. **Turn to 196.**

115

"I believe that Christopher Marshall is the murderer," you tell the three men watching you.

"Marshall?" McDonald asks in surprise. "How can that be? He helped us in the investigation and was one of the first men to insist that Watson was innocent when the evidence pointed against him."

"Patience, Mr. McDonald," Captain Locke says softly. "Surely the young man has proof for his charge, proof of motive, method and opportunity. Now almost anyone could have used that poker, if he could have been in the billiard room at nine o'clock. Can you prove that Marshall might have been there, that he had the opportunity to kill Sir Terrence?" You think over the evidence.

- *If you checked both Clue M and Clue O*, **turn to 300.**
- *If you checked Clue O*, **turn to 111.**
- *Otherwise*, **turn to 117.**

116

You try to think of any more questions you should ask Captain Lawrence. He is a man who obviously requires some careful handling.

- *If you checked Clue G*, **turn to 324.**
- *Otherwise*, **turn to 436.**

117

Locke listens to your explanation, then shakes his head. "You have no evidence that he had an opportunity," he says finally, "you must do better than that to prove a case."

- *If you begin the case again,* **turn to the Prologue.**
- *If you continue to try to prove Marshall's guilt,*
   turn to 318.

118

You call out from across the room: "Stop, thief!" Your warning is unheeded. *Turn to 591.*

You see splash marks in the dust near a small puddle and follow the wet footsteps around a corner. Marshall is obviously heading towards the river. You take off running again, hoping to catch him before he can board a boat and get away. **Pick a number** *and add your Athletics bonus:*

- *If 2-8,* **turn to 468.**
- *If 9-12,* **turn to 120.**

120

You come to a small waterway running down towards the Thames. A steam launch is just pulling out from a dock, and you see Marshall standing amidship. It is a small vessel with an open deck. Only the engine and boiler are protected by a roof. A powerfully built man stands near the back, working the wheel, while three other men are coiling ropes or doing other jobs around the deck. You have only a moment to decide how you can apprehend the killer.

- *If you try to jump onto the boat,* **turn to 122.**
- *Otherwise,* **turn to 468.**

121

You look at the three men, swallow hard, then manage to say: "I am sorry to be unworthy of your faith in me, gentlemen, but I have failed in the investigation. I do not know who killed Sir Terrence."

Mycroft tries to comfort you. "Do not worry, young man," he says heavily, "no man solves every case successfully. Even my brother failed on one or two occasions." **Turn to 525.**

122

You run down the pier and leap for the boat, trying to ignore the widening gap of water. You hope you jumped far enough to reach the launch. **Pick a number** *and add your Athletics bonus:*

- *If 2-7,* **turn to 317.**
- *If 8-12,* **turn to 191.**

123

As you stand outside your lodgings, you remember Symington, the man engaged in the same forms of crooked business promotion as Sir Terrence. You try to decide whether it would be worthwhile to visit the promoter.

- *If you see Symington,* **turn to 103.**
- *Otherwise,* **turn to 107.**

124

You hurry on to Mycroft Holmes's rooms to review the case with him and Inspector McDonald. You hope that you have learned enough to convince them both that Watson is innocent. Both men listen carefully as you explain the evidence that you have put together.

- *If you checked both Clue F and Clue Q,* **turn to 189.**
- *Otherwise,* **turn to 412.**

125

You remember the trapdoor in the floor of the billiard room and wonder whether Martin knew anything about it.

- *If you ask him about the trapdoor,* **turn to 340.**
- *Otherwise,* **turn to 570.**

126

You decide that no true detective would fail to investigate this exit. You squirm through it, with a disgusted Strickland following you, complaining all the way. You drop to the floor in an office with barred windows. A large safe stands in the corner. The door out of the room is locked. "Whose office is this?" you ask Strickland.

"This is the office of the club secretary," he answers. "We had bars put on the windows as we often have large amounts of money or other valuables in the safe. The secretary and I are the only ones who have keys to the door. Fortunately, I have mine with me, so I would not relish having to climb back through that silly trapdoor. There are no other secret exits from this room. We checked very thoroughly before we moved the safe in here." He opens the door and leads you into the hall by the stair that leads up to the billiard room. **Pick a number** *and add your Intuition bonus:*

- *If 2-7,* **turn to 277.**
- *If 8-12,* **turn to 378.**

127

Strickland is tapping his toes and is obviously very impatient with you. "Well, do you want to search anywhere else?" he asks sharply. "Perhaps there is evidence the murderer stepped into the fire and climbed up the chimney."

You look at the long curtains and wonder if someone behind them would be hidden from other people in the room.

- *If you ask Strickland to help,* **turn to 474.**
- *Otherwise,* **turn to 350.**

128

You look over Howard and wonder whether he has noticed anything that the other witnesses missed.

- *If you ask him to describe the evening,* **turn to 144.**
- *If you are through questioning him,* **turn to 129.**
- *Otherwise,* **turn to 429.**

129

You are satisfied that you have learned everything that John Howard knows. You thank him for his time and help, and he acknowledges you with a quick nod before leaving. **Turn to 407.**

130

You consider what other questions to ask Lord Howard. You wonder what he was doing when he heard Chambers' shouts of alarm.

- *If you ask him what he was doing,* **turn to 437.**
- *If you are through with him,* **turn to 561.**
- *Otherwise,* **turn to 508.**

131

You had always told yourself that you should learn how to swim, but you never bothered. Now it is too late. Weighed down by your clothes, you never make it to shore. An unnecessary drowning ends your promising career. **THE END.**

132

You try to think of more questions to ask Sir George and wonder if he knows anything else of use.

- *If you ask no more questions,* **turn to 333.**
- *Otherwise,* **pick a number** *and add your Intuition bonus:*
    - *If 2-6,* **turn to 184.**
    - *If 7-12,* **turn to 272.**

133

"Thank you for your time, your lordship," you begin. "As well as establishing what happened last night, I also am trying to understand why it happened."

"Yes?" he answers, puzzled.

You nod encouragingly. "Yes, my lord. What I would like you to tell me is what kind of man Sir Terrence was. This will give me some hint as to why he was murdered."

"Why he was murdered," the peer chuckles, "he was murdered because someone didn't like him. Now why they didn't, I'm not at all certain, for he was a nice enough fellow. He came from a good family of course—his father was made a baronet for service in the Crimea—and that should have helped him along. But he was a woefully bad businessman. A number of us lost money in his companies, but losing a few hundred pounds in a man's business is hardly grounds for bashing in his head." **Turn to 295.**

134

You try to decide who might be mentioned in Holmes' records. You wonder if he had any information on the Earl of Waynesborough. A glance at the indices show that the Earl is included in the collection.

- *If you look up the Earl,* **turn to 331.**
- *If you are finished investigating at Baker Street,*
     turn to 148.
- *Otherwise,* **turn to 465.**

135

"It's a very grim matter," you say slowly, and both McDonald and Mycroft nod in agreement.

"I admit to my own doubts of Watson's innocence," Mycroft adds. "But for Sherlock's sake I must see that there is action beyond the usual police investigation. I hope you are a fit choice." As he and McDonald chat a little more, you wonder why Watson hasn't been arrested.

- *If you ask McDonald this question,* **turn to 339.**
- *Otherwise,* **turn to 152.**

You stride up to Mrs. Hudson's house at 221 Baker Street and knock on the door. Mrs. Hudson, a very pleasant, motherly woman, answers the door herself.

"Hello," she says, in a delighted voice. "I remember you," she adds. "You used to work with Mr. Holmes. What are you doing now?"

"I am trying to pursue Mr. Holmes' old trade as a consulting detective," you answer. "I am currently looking into a rather important matter, and Mr. Mycroft Holmes was kind enough to give me permission to look at his brother's records." You show Mrs. Hudson the note.

After reading the note, Mrs. Hudson smiles and leads you upstairs. "I am pleased to have someone using Mr. Holmes' things," she mentions. "It seems so silly for Mr. Mycroft to pay me to maintain the rooms when he almost never has anyone use them. Occasionally his friend Captain Locke will come and use the books, but not often."

She lets you into the room, and you look around in surprise. If Holmes were alive, he could move back into Baker Street tomorrow. The sitting room is just as you remembered it, a comfortable room with big chairs, solid desks and tables, and all the other fittings for a bachelor's comfort. There is a large shelf by the fireplace, filled with Holmes' books, including the big scrapbooks he filled with clippings. You notice that Mrs. Hudson has replastered the wall Holmes had decorated with a patriotic V.R. in bullet marks. Without wasting more time, you sit to look into the records. With some effort, you find how the complicated indices correspond to the commonplace books, and then you begin to look up the people involved in this case. ***Check Clue U.***

- *If you look up Sir Terrence,* **turn to 158.**
- *Otherwise,* **turn to 134.**

137

Strickland scribbles away on his sheet of paper for a minute, then says, "The next man you might talk to is Mr. John Howard, a former naval officer and a member of this club. Do you wish to see him?"

- *If you talk to John Howard,* **turn to 192.**
- *Otherwise,* **turn to 407.**

138

You look at McDonald. "Inspector," you say, "this proves that Marshall was Symington's partner. As we know that he recommended Sir Terrence's companies to some of his friends, I think we can surmise that he was Sir Terrence's hidden partner as well. We had better go and arrest him at once." **Turn to 485.**

139

You cannot recognize the man and wonder what to do now. He may have nothing to do with the case. You know from checking the directory that Symington has the only occupied office on the upper floors, so this man must intend to see him.

- *If you go away and return in an hour,* **turn to 265.**
- *If you hide and wait for the man to leave,* **turn to 165.**
- *If you follow the man upstairs,* **turn to 584.**

140

You run onto the boat, even as it begins to move. A man who is obviously the captain grabs you by the shoulder and demands: "What the 'ell do you think you're doing, mister? This ain't no public excursion boat." Marshall is only a few feet away, staring at you in disbelief.

- *If you pull loose from the captain to seize Marshall,*
  turn to 145.
- *If you ask the captain to seize Marshall,* **turn to 572.**

141

As Watson congratulates you and thanks the captain, Inspector McDonald hurries to Baker Street to report to Mycroft Holmes and Captain Locke. **Turn to 591.**

142

"Did you know there was a trapdoor in the billiard room floor?" you ask.

"Oh is there?" Lord Howard answers. "No, you're just having a spot of fun with me, aren't you? This is a London Club, not some bizarre place out in the country. You had me believing you for a moment there." He chuckles at the very idea. **Turn to 561.**

143

You draw a deep breath, exhale, and then you and Strickland smile at each other. "I appreciate your cooperation," you tell Strickland. "I know it must have been a great strain for a busy man to pass an afternoon looking after an amateur detective."

"I hope the results prove worth the effort," he replies. "I like Dr. Watson, and while the evidence against him appears damning, I would be delighted if you proved that the facts can lie."

You thank Strickland for his help once again and leave the "Three Continents," tipping your hat to the doorman as you leave. You glance around on your way out. There are no empty cabs in sight, so you decide to walk to Mycroft's lodgings. A scattering of people move around, as the great city makes the transition from day to night. On a corner facing the club you notice a ragged looking man with a handful of papers in his hand, offering them to the other people hurrying along the street. **Pick a number** *and add your Intuition bonus:*

- *If 2-5,* **turn to 124.**
- *If 6-12,* **turn to 251.**

"Can you tell me what you saw happen last night?" you ask Howard.

"Of course I can, sir, of course I can," he replies. "That's what this is all about, isn't it? I understand that the problem began over cards, that Sir Terrence insulted Dr. Watson, and Dr. Watson knocked him down. I didn't see the fight myself, but I saw Sir Terrence, and you could see a lump swelling up right between his eyes. He chatted with some of us after it happened, then looked at the clock, excused himself, and went upstairs."

"And when was this?" you ask.

"Just before nine. He acted so much like a man with an appointment that I paid particular attention to the time myself. After he left, some of the rest of us stayed around talking until Chambers started screaming for help, after he had found the body." **Turn to 429.**

You try to shake off the captain's grip and go after Marshall, but the man is too strong. "What are you about?" he growls, shaking you. "Jonesy, Pete," he snaps, "help me throw this rat overboard." Two powerful crew men grab you and heave you into the water. **Turn to 317.**

You slow your stride. Marshall has a good lead. You might stand a better chance of intercepting him if you discern where he's going. **Pick a number** *and add your Scholarship bonus:*

- *If 2-5,* **turn to 147.**
- *If 6-8,* **turn to 151.**
- *If 9-12,* **turn to 173.**

You cannot imagine where Marshall might be going. You speed up, heading for the last place you saw him, and trying to watch for signs of his passage as you run. **Pick a number** *and add your Observation bonus:*

- *If 2-9,* **turn to 114.**
- *If 10-12,* **turn to 119.**

148

You put everything away, making sure that you leave the room just as you found it. Then you thank Mrs. Hudson for her help, bid her good day and leave Baker Street.

- *If you checked Decision 22,* **turn to 123.**
- *Otherwise,* **turn to 107.**

149

You follow Marshall, at the same time trying to keep him from realizing that he is being followed. You wonder where he is going. **Pick a number** *and add your Artifice bonus:*

- *If 2-7,* **turn to 373.**
- *If 8-12,* **turn to 483.**

150

You wonder whether he saw any sign that someone else was in the room besides Sir Terrence and Dr. Watson.

- *If you ask Chambers about signs of the presence of others,* **turn to 266.**
- *If you are through questioning him,* **turn to 439.**
- *Otherwise,* **turn to 507.**

151

From your knowledge of London, you know that Marshall is running towards the Thames. You recall that there is a small waterway nearby which feeds the river. Marshall probably has paid to have a steam launch waiting for him, in case of emergencies. You know the way to the nearest dock and run your fastest, hoping to catch him before his boat can pull out. **Pick a number** *and add your Athletics bonus:*

- *If 2-6,* **turn to 120.**
- *If 7-12,* **turn to 166.**

152

You consider other information that McDonald might provide. You wonder whether he can tell you anything useful about Sir Terrence's character.

- *If you ask McDonald about Sir Terrence,* **turn to 563.**
- *Otherwise,* **turn to 443.**

153

The men listen carefully as you explain matters. Mycroft and McDonald exchange glances, then nod. "You have found something," McDonald says. "I won't say that you have proven Watson innocent, but you have found some evidence that another man was hidden in the room while Watson was there. It will allow me to delay the arrest of Dr. Watson, pending further investigation." You sigh in relief—you have had some success in your investigation, at least. **Turn to 404.**

154

You step out the door and survey the new day. It is a pleasant, sunny morning, crisp but not cold. You stop for just a moment to consider what you should do first today.

- *If you checked Decision 17,* **turn to 502.**
- *Otherwise,* **turn to 345.**

155

"Now think as hard as you possibly can, man," you say, leaning towards Chambers. "You must remember whether that table was knocked over!"

Chambers flinches, then after a moment shakes his head. "No, sir," he says, "I just got no idea about any little table. How am I supposed to remember no little table when there was a poor man lying there dead? Please, Mr. Strickland," he adds, turning to the chairman, "don't let him do nought to me, just 'cause I can't remember his silly little table."

"There, there, Chambers, don't worry about it," Strickland says. "You may go now. The table is not important." Strickland turns to you and says, "And I'll thank you sir, not to abuse the members the way you abused poor Chambers, or I shall have you put out. But not until after the member you abuse gives you a good caning." **Turn to 515.**

156

McDonald looks briefly at the note, then says: "I've seen this code before, when Mr. Sherlock Holmes and I investigated the Birlstone murder. The numbers refer to words in some document or book, but there is no way to determine which book. It's not much help , though it does suggest that Symington had some dealings he kept secret." **Turn to 484.**

157

Mycroft breaks the silence with a cough, then asks you: "Well sir, now that you have learned everything we know about the suspects in the case, what will you do to pursue the matter? There is still a clever murderer on the loose, after all." You think about your course of action.

- *If you checked Clue I,* **turn to 473.**
- *If you checked Deduction 14, but not Clue I,* **turn to 187.**
- *Otherwise,* **turn to 213.**

158

Holmes has records on Sir Terrence. There are clippings describing the failure of the first two of his businesses. In a marginal note, Holmes says that Sir Terrence must have had a partner who furnished the money for the scheme, but the notes do not suggest the name of this partner. You consider whom else to read about in the books.

- *If you look up the Earl of Waynesborough,* **turn to 331.**
- *If you are finished at Baker Street,* **turn to 148.**
- *Otherwise,* **turn to 465.**

159

"Excuse me, Inspector," you say after a few moments thought. "Could you answer a few questions before I begin my investigation?"

"Certainly," McDonald replies, "I'm pleased to give you any help I may, sir. I'd be pleased to find that my reasoning is misguided."

- *If you ask him to discuss the timing of the murder more closely,* **turn to 418.**
- *Otherwise,* **turn to 456.**

"When you got up to the billiard room, what did you see?" you ask Johnson. "Do you remember anything odd?"

"Well," he answers quietly, "a dead baronet on the floor is not a common occurrence, even in this club, and the body distracted my attention from the surroundings. When Mr. Strickland and I ran in, there were a number of men clustered by the billiard table, and Dr. Watson was just standing up from the body. The doctor said Sir Terrence was dead just as we arrived."

- *If you checked Clue C,* **turn to 104.**
- *Otherwise,* **turn to 181.**

161

"What did you see, Mr. Howard," you ask, "when Chambers yelled and you ran upstairs?"

Howard thinks only a minute, then says: "All of us who were talking ran upstairs and into the billiard room. When we went in, Sullivan and Grant were in the room, standing, and Watson was kneeling over the body, making sure he was dead, I suppose. He'd waved the others back to protect the evidence, and Sullivan had backed off so much that I think he'd knocked over a little table, halfway across the room. Leastways, it was knocked over and Sullivan was standing close to it. I kept a close eye on Watson, from then on, because I wasn't sure whether he was trying to protect evidence or keep us back while he destroyed his traces."

- *If you ask who he was talking to downstairs,* **turn to 299.**
- *Otherwise,* **turn to 190.**

You find a trapdoor cleverly hidden in the floor beneath the billiard table, and point it out to Strickland. He looks surprised, then asks: "Are you going to waste the time to open it and see where it leads?" **Check Clue G.**

- *If you go through it,* **turn to 126.**
- *If you decide not to,* **turn to 336.**

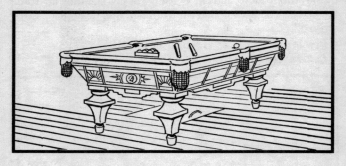

163

You take a deep breath, wondering if this is the right step, rise, and point straight at Marshall. He pauses, and looks back at you, a question in his eyes. Finally you speak. "Christopher Marshall," you begin, "you murdered Sir Terrence Milton last night. That is the only reason you could have to lie about this matter." Marshall, his face pale, stares at you in shock for a moment. The accusation is obviously the last thing he expected. **Pick a number** *and add your Communication bonus:*

- *If 2-10,* **turn to 355.**
- *If 11-12,* **turn to 576.**

164

You strike another match and look at the shelf carefully. It swings like a door, and you see a tunnel leading off under the back yard. You follow it, and find that it comes out under a shed in the back yard. A door in the back of the shed leads directly onto the street behind the house. **Check Clue Y. Turn to 323.**

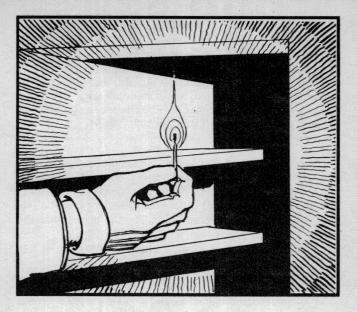

165

There are not many hiding places on a busy London street on a weekday morning. Finally, you pick up a newspaper and lean against the side of a building. You try to shield your face with the paper while you watch for Symington's visitor to leave. **Pick a number** *and add your Artifice bonus:*

- *If 2-7,* **turn to 316.**
- *If 8-12,* **turn to 342.**

166

As you approach the dock, you see Marshall run out of another roadway and onto a waiting boat. Immediately its crew begins to cast off the lines which hold the launch to the dock. It's obviously ready to go. You try to decide how to catch Marshall.

- *If you run onto the boat after him,* **turn to 140.**
- *If you watch it leave,* **turn to 468.**

167

"Thank you for your time," you tell Johnson. "Can you tell me anything about the fight in the card room last night, the one between Dr. Watson and Sir Terrence Milton?"

"There was a fight," he answers quietly, "but I don't know anything about it. The members of this club are a very lively group of men, and an outbreak of fisticuffs over cards is hardly a matter for comment." **Turn to 397.**

168

The oddity of the Baker Street rooms continues to trouble you. There is only one logical answer, but it seems impossible. The reports of Sherlock Holmes' death were definite, but you suddenly wonder if the great detective is still alive. That would be the only reason for his brother to maintain the Baker Street apartment.

- *If you ask if Sherlock is alive,* **turn to 237.**
- *Otherwise,* **turn to 244.**

169

You cannot see the man's face and wonder where he's going and what he is going to do. You see him turn down an alley and walk faster to catch up with him. When you turn down the alley, he has vanished from sight. The alley has the blank back wall of a building on one side and a high fence on the other. **Pick a number** *and add your Observation bonus:*

- *If 2-7,* **turn to 233.**
- *If 8-9,* **turn to 466.**
- *If 10-12,* **turn to 490.**

170

You idly flip through one or two of the Commonplace books, amazed at the amount of information that Sherlock Holmes had gathered over the years. Both the amount of material and the variety of the subject matter explain the great success enjoyed by the world's first consulting detective. Besides incidents in England, there are stories on such American events as the Borden murders in Massachusetts and the death of the Dalton Gang in Kansas, and crimes on every other continent. **Pick a number** *and add your Scholarship bonus:*

- *If 2-7,* **turn to 148.**
- *If 8-12,* **turn to 476.**

171

As the Inspector lifts the pieces of the bust from Symington's smashed cranium, you suddenly signal him to stop. You bend closer to the wound, then say excitedly: "Look, Inspector!" pointing to a laceration partially hidden by plaster dust. "Doesn't that look like a bullet wound?"

McDonald looks where you're pointing, then nods grimly. "Aye, lad," he answers. "The poor man was shot, and then the bust smashed on him to hide the wound. Shot in the back of the head; a cold-blooded murder." *Check Deduction 21.* **Turn to 353.**

172

"To understand why Sir Terrence was killed," you explain, "I need to understand what kind of man he was. Could you tell me what you knew of him?"

"Sir Terrence was a pleasant enough man," Howard replies, "though he could have a mean tongue in his head if he was irritated. A good clubman though, who was always willing to chat, or sit in on a hand of whist."

"Did you have any business dealings with him?" you ask.

"No, no," Howard answers, "That would not have been wise. When he ran a business big enough to be worth the effort of an investment, he ran it so badly that no sensible person would risk their money."

"So he was a poor businessman?" you ask.

"Yes, at least I hope he was," he answers. "If not, he was a villainous one. There were whispers about him, but nothing definite ever came of it. I enjoyed his companionship but avoided risking any money with him." **Pick a number** *and add your Intuition bonus:*

- *If 2-6,* **turn to 128.**
- *If 7-12,* **turn to 267.**

173

From your knowledge of London, you know that Marshall is running towards the Thames. You remember that there is a small waterway nearby which feeds the river. Perhaps Marshall has paid to have a steam launch waiting for him for just such an emergency. You know the way to the nearest dock and remember that the waterway runs under a footbridge before it reaches the Thames. As you run, you must decide where to go.

- *If you try to catch him at the boat,* **turn to 178.**
- *If you run to the bridge,* **turn to 509.**

174

Nodding to the bobby and the shopkeeper, you follow the man who visited Symington. You must hurry to keep him in sight, but at the same time you must avoid attracting attention. **Pick a number** *and add your Artifice bonus:*

- *If 2-8,* **turn to 169.**
- *If 9-12,* **turn to 424.**

175

"I am sorry if I gave offense," you say carefully. "Could you tell me what you saw and heard at the time of the murder?"

"I really have nothing useful to tell you," he answers stiffly. "I talked with some gentlemen down here until the servant began yelling about murder. Naturally we all ran upstairs, and saw the poor man lying there. Dr. Watson told us he was dead. I really don't know anything more I can say about it." It is so obvious that the Captain is angry with you that it doesn't seem worth the effort to ask him for more details. You wonder if you can get any useful information out of him.

- *If you checked Clue G,* **turn to 368.**
- *Otherwise,* **turn to 436.**

176

You come to "The Three Continents Club," located on a street leading off Pall Mall. From your knowledge of the city you decide that it was once the London residence of some noble or gentleman, probably sold to the club when the costs of modern living began to strain inherited incomes. On seeing

the letter from Inspector McDonald, the servant who answered the door leads you to the office of John Strickland, the
chairman of the club.

"I see that you are here to investigate that unfortunate affair
of last night," he says, and you can tell he's not overly pleased.
"Well, I hope this is the last of it. I'll have the butler assemble
the men who were here last night, so you can talk to them.
Meanwhile, I'll take you up to the billiard room and you can
see the scene of the crime. Though why you think you can find
something that the police missed, I cannot say."

After a word with a servant, Strickland leads you up a side
stair to a small hall with two or three rooms on each side. The
chairman tells you that only the billiard room, a small study
and the corner lavatory are used. A constable stands in front
of the billiard room, but he lets you in when the chairman
shows him McDonald's letter.

You step into the billiard room and glance around. *(You may
look at a map of the room at 205 at any time.)* The billiard

8

room is a snug place. Easy chairs flank a large fireplace, facing a sofa that stretches diagonally across the middle of the room. Drapes hanging from the ceiling to the floor hide three windows along the wall opposite the door. The billiard table fills one corner, with cue racks and other equipment near it. A cue lies across it, though the balls do not appear to have been broken by someone actually playing.

- *If you checked Clue C,* **turn to 273.**
- *Otherwise,* **turn to 245.**

177

You examine the body, suspicious of this odd accident. It seems a frightful coincidence that a man mentioned in your investigation has died so suddenly. **Pick a number** *and add your Observation bonus:*

- *If 2-5,* **turn to 288.**
- *If 6-12,* **turn to 188.**

178

You run quickly towards the dock, hoping to catch Marshall. **Pick a number** *and add your Athletics bonus:*

- *If 2-6,* **turn to 120.**
- *If 7-12,* **turn to 166.**

179

You have hopes when you see Symington's name in the indices, but there is only one small clipping in the books. It describes the first company promoted by Symington, but the story is only a paragraph. A note written in the margin reads, "Company sounds suspicious, no previous misbehaviour, no evidence." You return the book to the shelf. **Turn to 458.**

180

Locke shakes his head when you finish your explanations. "You have not proven a motive," he says. "I doubt a jury would convict him on the basis of the evidence. You must do better than this."

- *If you wish to begin again,* **turn to the Prologue.**
- *If you want an explanation of the case,* **turn to 499.**

181

You decide that you have learned all that you can learn from the butler. You thank him for answering your questions and bid him good day. **Turn to 447.**

182

You snap your fingers in delight as you remember how this kind of code works. There must be a document that provides the key for this message. If you number the words in the document, each number in the note will then translate into a word. And the most likely key document is the flyer for Sir Terrence's company. *(You may look at the flyer at* **204.***)* This would explain why Sir Terrence always kept a copy of it with him. **Turn to 479.**

183

"Captain! Captain!" you yell at the boat, "Stop at once!" The bulky commander looks up at you in surprise.

"Why should I?" he challenges you.

"That man is a murderer!" you say. "The police want him desperately." Marshall shakes his head vehemently and starts to speak to the captain. **Pick a number** *and add your Communication bonus:*

- *If 2-6,* **turn to 577.**
- *If 7-12,* **turn to 587.**

184

You consider further questions for Sir George and wonder whether anyone will provide any helpful comments on this case.

- *If you checked Clue C,* **turn to 230.**
- *If you have finished questioning Grant,* **turn to 333.**
- *Otherwise,* **turn to 351.**

185

You stand balanced on the edge of the bridge and try to drop onto the launch as it passes under you. **Pick a number** *and add your Athletics bonus:*

- *If 2-5,* **turn to 317.**
- *If 6-12,* **turn to 191.**

"You told the police that Dr. Watson went up to the billiard room just at nine," you say, and the butler nods. "How can you be so exact?"

The butler's shoulders lift in the slightest of shrugs. "I made a point of remembering after the body was found," he answers. "The doctor came to me and asked for a good stiff brandy, as he needed to settle his temper a little, and he mentioned the fight with Sir Terrence. When I served his brandy, he told me he was going to the billiard room to read the paper and calm down a little. He left the hall door open and I saw him start up the steps, just as the clock in the smoking room chimed the hour. That is a clock that we are always careful to keep on the correct time. The inspector verified that this morning, after he interviewed me." **Turn to 260.**

187

Sighing deeply and weary from the long day, you try to think of other sources of information in this case. **Pick a number** *and add your Intuition bonus:*

- *If 2-7,* **turn to 542.**
- *If 8-12,* **turn to 248.**

188

When you examine the body, you find that the fallen bust obscures a bullet wound. Symington has been shot in the back of the head. You try to decide what to do now. *Check Decision 21.*

- *If you send for the police immediately,* **turn to 391.**
- *If you search the office,* **turn to 428.**

189

You explain the evidence carefully, hoping it is as convincing to Mycroft and McDonald as it seems to you. "You see," you say in summary. "The vendor saw a man hiding between the curtains and the window, and I confirmed that he would be hidden from anyone in the room. The man was in there all the time that Watson was in the room. Obviously, he must be the murderer. He killed Sir Terrence, and before he could leave, he heard Watson coming down the hall so he had to hide."

Mycroft nods heavily, obviously pleased. "Your investigation is a great relief to me," he says. "I was afraid that Inspector McDonald would arrest Watson this evening. Now, it would seem that the Doctor may very well be innocent, and that the hidden man committed the murder." *Check Deduction 10.* **Turn to 404.**

190

You try to think of other questions that you should ask Howard. What useful things might he know?

- *If you checked Clue G,* **turn to 510.**
- *Otherwise,* **turn to 129.**

191

You land on the launch, though somewhat awkwardly. While a shocked Marshall watches, a burly man pulls you to your feet. "What the 'ell do you think you're doing?" he screams into your face. "I've no time for that sort of trick. I should 'eave you overboard!" You have only a moment to decide what to do.

- *If you try to pull free and grab Marshall,* **turn to 145.**
- *If you ask the captain to seize Marshall,* **turn to 141.**

192

John Howard comes in. He is a big, hard-faced man, who has grown fat since his days in the navy. He carries the weight easily, however, and his sharp eyes suggest that self-indulgence has not slowed up his mind.

"Thank you for staying to talk with me," you begin. "I know you must be a busy man, Mr. Howard."

"Not too busy to oblige Mr. Strickland," he answers, "though it's all pretty much a waste of time, isn't it? I gathered that the evidence points straight at John Watson." You wonder what parts of the case he can help you understand.

- *If you ask his opinion of Sir Terrence,* **turn to 172.**
- *Otherwise,* **turn to 128.**

Symington looks very carefully at you. "If I tell you, will you promise not to repeat what I say?" You nod in affirmation.

Symington pauses to think, then finally says: "Very well. There is a man named Christopher Marshall, who helped both Sir Terrence and myself. He loaned me money, and I paid him back tenfold. He'd also advise some of his friends to invest with us. He wouldn't listen to me when I told him Sir Terrence was too big a fool to trust. It's fortunate for both of us that Sir Terrence was murdered before he could talk too much."
Check Deduction 27. **Turn to 438.**

You wrack your own brains, trying to think of a good way to trigger Chambers' memory and prove whether the little table was knocked over. **Pick a number** *and add your Intuition bonus:*

- *If 2-6,* **turn to 500.**
- *If 7-12,* **turn to 578.**

Locke looks at you and McDonald, an intent look in his grey eyes. "You gentlemen must go and arrest Marshall. McDonald, you and our friend should go out to Marshall's house in the morning. Good hunting."

It is barely seven the next morning when McDonald bangs on your door. You are dressed and ready as you head west to Marshall's home. **Turn to 338.**

You and McDonald take a hansom to Pall Mall to report your failure. You wish the trip were a hundred miles instead of two. After you climb the steps to Mycroft's rooms and knock, Mycroft opens the door, sighing when he sees you. "So he got away," he says. "Well, come in and tell us how the rogue managed it. I would have preferred to have him in a cell confessing, to be certain that Watson is cleared. Still, the police might catch him when he tries to leave the country."

Slowly, embarassed by your failure, you explain how Marshall got away.

- *If you checked Decision 26,* **turn to 199.**
- *Otherwise,* **turn to 202.**

197

"Did you know that there was a trapdoor in the billiard room?" you ask Lewis.

For a moment he sits as though thunderstruck, then shakes himself and smiles. "My," he says, "there is some truth to the stories they tell about you detectives, isn't there. Fancy you finding that. I hadn't thought of that trapdoor in twenty years. When I was a boy, my father would bring me here when he visited the Earl of Waynesborough, and Lord Grayson and I would play many a game involving that trapdoor. I don't know that I could find it myself anymore." *Check Deduction 7 and Deduction 29.* **Turn to 311.**

198

The constables pound on the door and get no reaction. After waiting a few minutes, McDonald forces the back door and searches the house. He comes out shaking his head. "The bird is flown," he tells you. "Something must have made him fear that we knew, and he left without wasting a second. From the look of the house, he took nothing but the barest necessities and whatever cash he had on hand." **Turn to 196.**

199

Locke listens to your explanation, then shakes his head regretfully. "So the fox was gone when you got there," he says. "I wonder why he fled." He pauses to think, then asks you: "When you searched his house, did you take special care that everything was put away properly?"

You shake your head. "No sir," you reply. "I did not want to risk Marshall catching me in his house. He must have seen signs of my search and fled at once."

Locke nods. "When you have narrowed your investigation to one or two men, you must not let them know you suspect them. Do not scare a man into running unless you have the net spread for him as he flees. But you will do better in your next case." **THE END.**

200

You throw open the door and rush into the room. Marshall spins around while Symington dives to the floor. With Marshall's gun pointed at you, you desperately leap to one side to escape its threat. Before you can make a move to tackle Marshall, he races out the door. You hear his steps thundering down the stair.

"Thank God you were there!" Symington says, rising from the floor. "He'd have murdered me otherwise." **Turn to 546.**

201

You recall that your two colleagues mentioned a man named Symington as a possible killer, then dismissed him.

- *If you ask for information on Symington,* **turn to 579.**
- *Otherwise,* **turn to 445.**

202

McDonald explains that the hidden tunnel from his house allowed Marshall to get away. "Then he had that launch with her fires up waiting for him, Captain," he adds, "and we just weren't quick enough to catch him."

Locke nods. "Marshall is a sly fox," he admits. "I should have told you that he is fond of hidden tunnels and secret exits. He wrote a monograph on the subject. Well, you will not make the same mistake again. Your next case shall be an even greater success." As Mycroft presides over a light meal he has had prepared for you, you think over those magic words — your next case. What adventures await? **THE END.**

203

Sullivan is tall and heavily-built, but also seems alert, sharp-eyed and observant. He politely acknowledges Strickland's introduction of you, then sits back to wait for your questions.

"I should like you to tell me what happened last night," you say to Sullivan. "Take all the time you need, and tell me what you saw and heard."

Sullivan smiles, then begins: "I have heard I missed a major part of the excitement, as Watson and Sir Terrence had a good fight downstairs first. But I knew nothing of what happened until Chambers began to scream. As you probably know, I was playing chess with Sir George Grant, and we both ran out into the hall and followed Chambers into the billiard room. Chambers pointed to where Sir Terrence was lying, and we stood around talking about what could have happened, especially after the other members came in. I glanced around as I came into the room, but I didn't see anyone in there who could have killed Milton."

- *If you ask what Watson did after the alarm,* **turn to 314.**
- *If you are finished with Sullivan,* **turn to 448.**
- *Otherwise,* **turn to 337.**

204

The Ivory Coast Mining Venture

The Ivory Coast Mining Venture is the most promising speculative venture to be offered to the public in many a year. The legendary wealth of the Ivory Coast, known to informed men for a thousand years, can now be exploited again. A few investors can share in this wealth, men willing to speak out and take a risk to win wealth. Those who turn away, silent and cautious when the hour calls for daring, will never be great.

The most daring men in Europe first journeyed to the Ivory Coast to trade for gold. The easy wealth of the slave trade distracted them from tracing the actual mines. Study of the most ancient documents has located the mines. The discovery has been confirmed by the native storytellers of local tribes, men who have kept alive the history of their people, telling stories that have been passed down from father to son for hundreds of years.

Come you sons of England, marshall your courage for the new challenge! We, the managers of the company, know that any true man who has read this far will be more than willing to risk his money with us in this venture. Join us! Meet with us so we can explain the details of this venture. A chance of this sort comes only once in your life.

Sir Terrence Milton, Chairman
Mr. Robert Cotton, Secretary

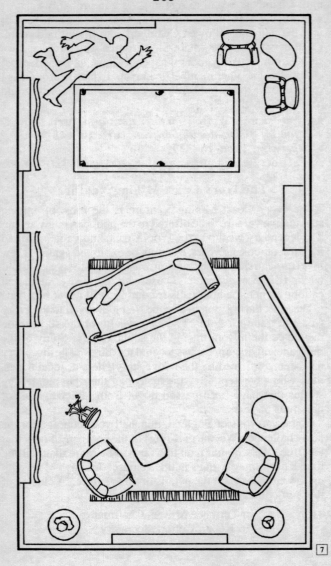

206

"You say Watson left the room?" you ask Marshall. "That is odd. Someone told me you took him out of the room."

Marshall smiles. "Oh, you detectives," he says in jest, "you will jump onto any slight difference in men's stories. I made certain that Watson was clear of the room and then came back and chatted with the others until Chambers began yelling about the murder." *Check Clue M.*

- *If you checked Clue O*, **turn to 503.**
- *Otherwise*, **turn to 308.**

207

You wonder what opinion Strickland had of Sir Terrence.

- *If you ask his opinion*, **turn to 472.**
- *If you are through with him*, **turn to 228.**
- *Otherwise*, **turn to 555.**

208

In spite of his efforts, you manage to keep Marshall in sight. He heads for a waterway near the Thames and runs onto a waiting steam launch. The crew immediately begins to cast loose the ropes and prepares to leave. You wonder what to do now.

- *If you let the boat leave*, **turn to 468.**
- *If you run onto the boat after Marshall*, **turn to 140.**

209

9   9:00

230	205	ME	25	40	164
113	IF	162	139	71	213
WHEN	173	205	126	234	2
15	200	117	WHY	166	SAFE

"Think back on when you were sitting in the room," you tell Watson. "Did you notice that a small table was knocked over?"

"A small table?" he asks in return. "No, I can't say I remember any such thing. And if there had been, I would have picked it up. Can't have the furniture tipped over, you know, not in your own club." **Turn to 332.**

"How did Watson react to all this?" you ask. "Did he seem his normal self?"

"Come now, sir," Grant answers. "No man would seem his normal self with a murdered man lying on the floor. But Watson did seem shocked. He said he had been in the room for half an hour, and he couldn't understand how Sir Terrence came to be lying there like that. He cooled down after looking at the body though. I think carrying out your professional duties steadies a man down in a crisis, and he mentioned that Milton had been dead for a while, that he must have been lying there when Watson came into the room."

"Did you believe him?" you ask.

"I didn't know what to believe," he answers. "I asked John if he had done it, and he said he hadn't. Very indignant at the very idea, of course." **Turn to 132.**

You go over the fine wood floor of the room, looking everywhere for a possible trap door. The task is complicated by the small, colorful rugs scattered around the room. **Pick a number** *and add your Observation bonus:*

- *If 2-8,* **turn to 326.**
- *If 9-12,* **turn to 162.**

"This note business is all very well," Mycroft says, "but does it tell us anything important about the case?"

"I cannot say that it does," McDonald answers. "In fact it is worse than that, as far as you are concerned."

"What do you mean?" Mycroft asks.

"Well, obviously, this note could point directly at Dr. Watson," McDonald says. "I learned of this sort of code when I investigated the Birlstone case with your brother. Obviously, Watson could have learned it at the same time. If the note is an appointment to meet Sir Terrence, who would be more likely to have sent the note than a man who went up to the billiard room just after Sir Terrence? Some would suggest that he kept his appointment and then murdered Sir Terrence." **Turn to 247.**

214

The Earl seems to think about the case, then shakes his head. "I don't wish to speculate about the matter," he finally says. "I know that some men disliked him, but I don't know that any of them hated him enough to murder him."

"Could you name some of his enemies?" you urge.

"No, I don't think that I should," he answers. "I have no evidence, and I know that I would deeply resent any man describing me as a possible murderer. I think I've said enough." **Turn to 441.**

215

"So you did not invest with Sir Terrence," you continue. "Do you know if your fellow members shared your opinion of Sir Terrence's skills? Did others in the club invest with him?"

"Did they share my views?" he answers, laughing harshly. "It would be a boring club indeed if all the members shared the same views on such matters. No, I think he convinced a number of them to invest with him. He knew how to make his companies sound good, even if he didn't know how to make them work once the money was collected."

"Do you know who invested with him?" you continue.

"Oh, a number of the chaps did," he answers. "Dr. Watson lost something on his last company, the Earl of Waynesborough was another of them, and I believe Alexander Lewis actually made the mistake of trusting Sir Terrence twice. And of course, there's Christopher Marshall. I'm certain he must have invested a good bit with Sir Terrence. He certainly urged enough other people to do so." *Check Deductions 8 and 13.* **Turn to 128.**

"Can you remember how you heard of his venture?" you ask.

"Oh, I don't know," he answers. "I must have heard some talk of it around the club." He pauses a moment. "Oh, I know, I had told my friend Marshall that I was looking for a good investment, and he told me that Sir Terrence was putting a company together. Marshall was very upset that the investment turned out badly." *Check Clue E*. **Turn to 332.**

217

"You were downstairs talking when you heard of the murder," you say slowly, making a show of checking your notes, and Lawrence nods impatiently. "Do you remember to whom you were talking?" you ask.

He thinks for a minute or so, as though ordering the facts very carefully in his mind. "When the servant screamed I was talking to two men," he says finally, "Lord Howard and Mr. Howard. There had been some others in the conversation, but they left for engagements of their own. The three of us ran upstairs together when the servant started screaming." *Check Clue O*. **Turn to 569.**

218

You follow Marshall down the street, staying far enough back to avoid being noticed. He walks two or three blocks, then stops and calls a cab. The only hansom in sight picks him up and then rattles on.

- *If you return to see Symington,* **turn to 234.**
- *Otherwise,* **turn to 520.**

219

"Johnson," you continue, "Would you please tell me what you were doing when you heard about the murder?"

He almost smiles at the question. "Begging your pardon, heard is the right word, sir. Bobby Chambers ran out into the upstairs hall yelling 'MURDER!' at the top of his lungs. When that happened, Mr. Strickland and I were in the dining room, making certain that everything was laid out properly for the late supper buffet. We both ran upstairs, naturally." **Turn to 496.**

220

A step creaks under you and you hesitate, but the other man's footsteps never stop. You then believe him to be in the hallway. When you hear a door open, you go up and stand outside Symington's office.

You cannot understand everything that is being said in the office, but the conversation doesn't sound unfriendly. Finally you hear sounds of the talk breaking up. You walk down to the end of the hall, and watch the doorway over the top of your paper. A few seconds later Marshall exits and goes downstairs. *Check Clue T.*

- *If you follow Marshall,* **turn to 218.**
- *If you talk to Symington,* **turn to 477.**

221

"I believe that the Earl of Waynesborough murdered Sir Terrence," you say. "He had the motive, as Sir Terrence cheated him and also made uncouth advances to the Earl's wife. And the Earl once owned the club's building. He would have been able to find a place to hide, and then to get away when everyone else fussed over the body."

The others listen to your explanation, then shake their heads. McDonald explains: "The Earl would have had to be in London to commit the crime. I have made inquiries, and he never left his manor that evening. He could not have done it." **Turn to 525.**

222

You cock an ear when Marshall comments that Watson left the room after the fight, as someone told you that Marshall took Watson out of the room. You wonder if Marshall can explain this seeming discrepancy.

- *If you ask Marshall about the problem,* **turn to 206.**
- *If you are done with Marshall,* **turn to 405.**
- *Otherwise,* **turn to 112.**

223

You begin a systematic examination of Symington's desk, opening each drawer and checking the contents. While there are papers dealing with his business and a wide variety of letters on differenct subjects, there is no evidence to identify any secret partners in his operations. **Pick a number** *and add your Artifice bonus:*

- *If 2-6,* **turn to 469.**
- *If 7-12,* **turn to 478.**

224

Trying to choose your words carefully, you ask Watson; "Mr. McDonald mentioned that Sir Terrence insulted a lady during the argument. Could that be relevant in this affair?" **Pick a number** *and add your Communication bonus:*

- *If 2-8,* **turn to 375.**
- *If 9-12,* **turn to 427.**

225

Realizing that this will probably be your only chance to locate relevant evidence from Symington's office, you decide to search the desk. You go through all the papers and other items in it, but fail to find anything of use. You look the desk over again. There must be something useful in this room. **Pick a number** *and add your Artifice bonus:*

- *If 2-7,* **turn to 280.**
- *If 8-12,* **turn to 419.**

226

"I hope to find evidence of the killer in Sir Terrence's papers," you explain. "If no one has examined them yet, I would appreciate it if you would let me look through them."

"The police did not care," Perkins answers, rubbing a little at an eye. "You look at his papers and take all the time you need." He leads you into a study and points out where Sir Terrence kept his records. "You just makeyourself comfortable, sir, and I'll get you a pot of tea." **Turn to 575.**

227

Using a trick taught to you by Holmes when you were still a Baker Street Irregular, you pry open the window. Certain that no one can see you, you slip through the opening into the basement, and then latch the window behind you. Lighting a match, you look around. **Pick a number** *and add your Observation bonus:*

- *If 2-7,* **turn to 323.**
- *If 8-12,* **turn to 541.**

228

"Thank you for answering my questions," you say to Strickland, realizing you will learn nothing more from him. "You have been a great help in my investigation." **Turn to 352.**

229

You consider whether Lord Howard knows anything more that may be of use, and whether he can remember it if he does.

- *If you don't want to ask him anything,* **turn to 561.**
- *If you checked Clue C,* **turn to 289.**
- *Otherwise,* **turn to 508.**

230

"When you went into the room, did you notice whether one of the little tables was knocked over?" you ask.

"Table?" Grant answers vaguely. "I didn't look around the room; I was too busy looking at poor Milton. Ghastly sight!" **Turn to 351.**

231

A hansom takes you and McDonald to Pall Mall, and you quickly go up to Mycroft's rooms. He smiles when he opens his door. "I could tell from your knock that you have captured the rogue," he says. "Congratulations! Come in, and tell Captain Locke and me all about the pursuit."

Mycroft has tea and a light meal prepared for you. He and Captain Locke listen carefully to the story of your pursuit. You bask in the glory of your success, but at the same time you are already beginning to wonder what your next case will be. **THE END.**

232

You decide that it would be less than tactful to ask Watson about the lady but wonder if he has any theories about who killed Sir Terrence.

- *If you ask him who might have killed Sir Terrence,* **turn to 442.**
- *Otherwise,* **turn to 263.**

233

Without a clue or word of warning, a heavy stick crashes down across the back of your head, and you fall unconscious to the pavement.

You regain consciousness in a hospital bed and are surprised to see Inspector McDonald sitting beside it.

"Well, lad," he says, "you finally woke up. Someone struck you a shrewd blow indeed. Do you know who did it?"

- *If you checked Clue T,* **turn to 106.**
- *Otherwise,* **turn to 423.**

234

You return to Symington's office, trying to decide what business Marshall might have had with him. You wonder if your noise on the steps caught Marshall's attention and changed his course of action. As you come to Symington's street, you see a man hurry out of his door, a bulging valise in his hand. Before you can talk to him, the man catches a cab and rides away.

Wondering if this was Symington, you hurry up the stairs to his office. The door is open, and the simple room looks as if a whirlwind has struck. The file and desk drawers are open, and several books have been strewn across the floor. Evidently Symington packed and fled as quickly as he could. You search his office with great care, but find nothing of interest. **Turn to 315.**

235

You must decide whether it is useful to ask Martin further questions. He cannot tell you anything about the scene in the Billiard Room because he left before the body was discovered.

- *If you checked Clue G,* **turn to 125.**
- *Otherwise,* **turn to 570.**

236

"Hear anything?" he answers. "No, I can't say whether I heard anything or not. We were concentrating on the game, of course." *Check Clue K.* **Turn to 184.**

237

"Mr. Holmes," you ask Mycroft, "this question may ruin your confidence in my faculties, but I feel I must ask it. Is your brother Sherlock alive?"

Mycroft sits very still, as though shocked by your question, and at a loss for an answer. Then he looks sharply at both you and Captain Locke. "What I am going to tell you is a secret," he finally says, "and I want both of you to promise not to reveal what I say to anyone, especially Dr. Watson, until you are given permission."

Impressed by his seriousness, you and Locke hastily agree to his demand. "Very well," Mycroft says, "you have uncovered one of the most carefully protected secrets in the whole of England. My brother Sherlock Holmes is alive, though he is in hiding in France. While most of the men involved in his last case are dead or imprisoned, one of the most dangerous could not be charged with any crime. The man has sworn to kill my brother. While that man is at large, my brother cannot be seen in London. Not even Sherlock could safely walk about the streets of London, knowing that the most skilled rifle shot in the entire British Empire wished to kill him. Until that man makes a mistake that permits his arrest, Sherlock cannot return."

"But if his enemy knows Sherlock is still alive, why must he pretend to be dead?" you ask, puzzled.

"It is the price of fame," Locke answers. "Others would hunt out Mr. Holmes, if they knew he was alive, and they would lead the killer to his door." **Pick a number** *and add your Observation bonus:*

- *If 2-8,* **turn to 244.**
- *If 9-12,* **turn to 430.**

238

You recall that Watson's friend Marshall lied to you. You wonder whether Holmes had any notes on Marshall.

- *If you want to look up Marshall,* **turn to 512.**
- *Otherwise,* **turn to 170.**

239

Strickland gets up and takes a turn or two across the room, stretching his arms a little as he does it. After this brief bit of exercise he returns to his chair, picks up his list and tells you that Alexander Lewis is the next witness.

- *If you talk to Lewis,* **turn to 568.**
- *Otherwise,* **turn to 306.**

240

Given his certainty that Watson is innocent of the murder, you wonder whether Sullivan suspects anyone.

- *If you ask whom he suspects,* **turn to 426.**
- *If you are through with him,* **turn to 448.**
- *Otherwise,* **turn to 337.**

241

Though you look over the table and the outline of the body behind it, you find nothing more of interest. **Turn to 558.**

242

You rise early the next day, breakfast quickly, and set out on your day's investigation. You are anxious to get down to business. Today's work will show whether or not you can solve this murder. You try to decide what you should do first today.

- *If you checked both Deduction 14 and Decision 17,* **turn to 536.**
- *Otherwise,* **turn to 154.**

243

"Well, do you have any other questions?" Watson snaps, obviously irritated.

"Do you have any idea who would have wanted to kill Sir Terrence?" you ask. **Pick a number** *and add your Communication bonus:*

- *If 2-9,* **turn to 425.**
- *If 10-12,* **turn to 461.**

244

You thank Mycroft and Locke for their help and detail your plans for the investigation. Mycroft listens and nods, while Locke watches from a corner, hardly paying attention.

"Come back to see me as soon as you finish," Mycroft urges. "I will have McDonald here this evening, and I think Captain Locke should be here as well. Between us, we ought to be able to interpret the evidence." You leave his lodgings, eager to pursue the remainder of your investigation.

- *If you go to see Sir Terrence's lodging,* **turn to 559.**
- *Otherwise,* **turn to 262.**

245

You look carefully around the billiard room before making a close examination of the area where the body was found. **Pick a number** *and add your Observation bonus:*

- *If 2-8,* **turn to 497.**
- *If 9-12,* **turn to 250.**

246

You wonder if Lewis knows anything else of interest. It is useless to ask him about the murder scene, of course, as he had left the club before the body was discovered.

- *If you checked Clue G,* **turn to 102.**
- *Otherwise,* **turn to 311.**

247

As you consider the evidence, Mycroft and McDonald ask if there is anything else they can tell you. You contemplate the question. **Pick a number** *and add your Intuition bonus:*

- *If 2-6,* **turn to 187.**
- *If 7-12,* **turn to 539.**

248

"Mr. Holmes," you begin, a little shy, "I remember from my days as an irregular that your brother kept huge indices and scrapbooks, filled with information on men in every walk of life in London. Do they still exist?"

Mycroft looks surprised at the question, then nods. "Yes, they are still in his old rooms on Baker Street. I've paid Mrs. Hudson to keep them for me. Some day, when the needs of the country are less pressing, I shall go through the material and decide what to do with it."

"Could you give me a note for Mrs. Hudson, allowing me look in your brothers' commonplace books?" you ask. "They might be a useful source of information."

Mycroft hesitates again, then nods firmly. He scribbles a note and hands it to you. "Sherlock would certainly approve of his files being used to help Dr. Watson," he says. *Check Decision 14.* **Turn to 542.**

249

In spite of your efforts you cannot open the stubborn window. You study it and shake your head. Even if you dared risk the noise and smash the glass, you couldn't fit in because of the heavy frame. Feeling embarassed you slip over the wall and steal away. At least the police didn't catch you in your attempt at burglary. **Turn to 560.**

You notice that the little table beside the more distant easy chair has been knocked over, and wonder when this happened. *Check Clue C*. **Turn to 259.**

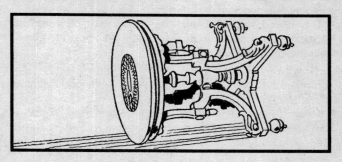

251

You wonder if the man works from the same corner every evening. If so, he might have seen something useful the night before. You walk near him, and he holds out a flyer for one of the music halls.

"This is the show you should see!" he says urgently, as you look at the flyer. "Best show in all London, three performances a night, at seven, nine and eleven."

- *If you stop to talk to the man,* **turn to 462.**
- *Otherwise,* **turn to 124.**

252

You think back on the other evidence you've seen, and you suddenly remember that Sir Terrence repaid a loan of 3000 pounds to Marshall. The check shows that Marshall only loaned him three hundred. After a little thought you understand. Marshall provided Sir Terrence with the money to promote his company. In return, Marshall received a major share of the illicit profits of the fraudulent scheme. Marshall and Sir Terrence were actually partners! *Check Deduction 27*. **Turn to 348.**

253

"Look at it, Inspector," you say, the excitement showing in your voice. "Isn't it similar to the code on the note I found in the billiard room? The handwriting is similar too — I remember the fours on the other note were very oddly made."

"It is indeed, lad," McDonald agrees, pleased. "No way to interpret it this time, though. I couldn't even begin to guess what the key to the code could be."

"Still, it proves that Sir Terrence and Symington must have dealt with the same man," you say. "A hidden partner!" **Check Clue R.**

- *If you checked Deduction 21,* **turn to 464.**
- *Otherwise,* **turn to 454.**

254

Locke listens to your explanation, thinks about it, then nods very slowly. "Yes," he finally says, "that does indicate that Marshall could have been Milton's partner. With Sir Terrence under investigation, a man might kill to protect himself from prosecution as a partner in fraud."

- *If you checked Clue S,* **turn to 372.**
- *Otherwise,* **turn to 195.**

255

Captain Lawrence glares at you, his ramrod spine growing even stiffer. "Sir," he says sharply, "when Captain Edward Lawrence of Her Majesty's Engineers says that he knows nothing of some matter, he knows nothing of the matter. And I resent the very suggestion that I would tell anything but the truth. I can see that you have little future as a detective." He is so angry that you hesitate to ask him further questions.

- *If you ask him what he saw and heard during the murder,* **turn to 175.**
- *Otherwise,* **turn to 585.**

256

"Recalling what you knew of him, what do you think of Sir Terrence?" you ask Watson. "What sort of man was he?" **Pick a number** *and add your Communication bonus:*

- *If 2-7,* **turn to 566.**
- *If 8-12,* **turn to 556.**

257

"When did you hear of the fight?" you ask.

"I heard of it when we were upstairs with the body," Strickland replies, after thinking for a minute. "We were all quite taken aback at seeing poor Sir Terrence dead, and then Christopher Marshall said something like: 'Really a bad evening for the poor fellow—first John Watson knocks him down and then someone else beats his head in!' From the look of things Watson may have done both." **Turn to 301.**

258

"Sir Terrence," Symington says thoughtfully. "You seem a discreet young man to me," he then pauses. "What I say won't go any further, will it?"

"If that is your wish, sir," you answer.

Symington nods. "Very well. I despised Sir Terrence, to state the matter plainly. He gave himself airs, because his father was a baronet, but he was a scoundrel. And worse than that, he was stupid. Most of us who promote high-risk companies take a certain care to at least attempt to operate the company. Sir Terrence would say there was a company, wait a few months, and then announce its failure. Such a man is dangerous to men like me, as the police are seldom satisfied with the arrest of one culprit. After they had caught him they would have looked into many another man's affairs. If I didn't object to murder on principle, I'd be pleased by his death." *Check Deduction 24.*

- *If you ask him about Sir Terrence's partners,* **turn to 410.**
- *If you ask nothing more,* **turn to 438.**

259

You walk over to the little table and look around. The table itself is nothing out of the ordinary, but you can see the outline of the body chalked on the floor beyond the billiard table. If the table were knocked over by Watson while he was in the room, he certainly would have seen the body. **Turn to 275.**

260

You wonder whether Johnson knows anything more worth the time to question him.

- *If you ask where he was when he heard of the murder,* **turn to 219.**
- *If you have finished questioning him,* **turn to 181.**
- *Otherwise,* **turn to 496.**

261

"I understand that Sir Terrence was a rival of yours," you begin. "What sort of man was he? You know they say a man's rivals often know more about him than his friends." **Pick a number** *and add your Communication bonus:*

- *If 2-7,* **turn to 552.**
- *If 8-12,* **turn to 258.**

262

You try to order events in your mind. Where else might you find evidence for this case?

- *If you checked Deduction 19, Clue S, or Clue X,* **turn to 293.**
- *Otherwise,* **turn to 560.**

263

"Thank you for your time, Doctor," you say quietly. "I assure you that I will do everything in my power to find the man who killed Sir Terrence. But whatever the evidence, not even the police believe you killed the man." As you leave the doctor's house, you ponder your next action.

Remembering Mycroft Holmes's advice, you go to visit Watson's friend Marshall, but you find he is not home. You will have to talk to him later at the club. From his house you go on to the "Three Continents" Club. **Turn to 176.**

264

You decide that a little background knowledge will aid your investigation. You therefore set out walking towards Baker Street, enjoying the morning sunshine. *Check Decision 22.* **Turn to 136.**

265

You knock on the door of Symington's office and get no answer. You knock again with no response. Surprised, you test the knob. It isn't locked, but you wonder whether you should enter the office without permission.

- *If you go in,* **turn to 565.**
- *Otherwise,* **turn to 315.**

266

"Did you see any sign of anyone else in the room?" you ask Chambers. "Anyone besides Sir Terrence and Dr. Watson? Signs like other glasses or anything else?"

"Oh, there was nothing of that type," he says. "The only glass was Dr. Watson's. I'm glad I didn't see no one, of course," he adds, "because anyone hidden there must have been the killer, and if I seen him, he would have killed me." **Turn to 507.**

267

You wonder whether the other members of the "Three Continents" shared Howard's views of Sir Terrence's business skills.

- *If you ask if other members invested with Sir Terrence,* **turn to 215.**
- *Otherwise,* **turn to 128.**

268

After hearing every argument you can make from the evidence, McDonald rises and shakes his head. "I am very sorry," he says, "but I cannot delay the arrest any longer on the basis of the evidence you found. I must arrest Dr. Watson tonight." He rises and leaves, and you follow despondently. You have failed in your investigation. *You may return to the Prologue and attempt the case again.* **THE END.**

269

You wonder if Holmes' had any notes on that other unscrupulous businessman, John Symington.

- *If you look up Symington,* **turn to 179.**
- *If you are prepared to leave Baker Street,* **turn to 148.**
- *Otherwise,* **turn to 458.**

270

After a little more talk, you realize that you've learned everything useful that McDonald and Mycroft know about the Earl of Waynesborough. You think about the other suspects and wonder if you can learn anything about them from their colleagues.

- *If you ask about Lewis,* **turn to 494.**
- *Otherwise,* **turn to 201.**

271

Lord Howard immediately gives you the impression that he is fortunate to have an inherited income. Though tall and handsome, with distinguished-looking grey hair, the peer obviously is not the wisest man in London. He has the calm assumption of superiority which the aristocracy often substitutes for intelligence. You doubt that he observed the details of the evening's events, but he might have a useful opinion of the late Sir Terrence.

- *If you ask his opinion of Sir Terrence,* **turn to 133.**
- *Otherwise,* **turn to 295.**

272

"When did your chess game begin?" you ask Grant.

"We began to play about eight," Sir George answers. "We drew our first game and started another immediately."

"Did you hear anything out of the ordinary before Chambers called out?" you continue. **Pick a number** *and add your Communication bonus:*

- *If 2-6,* **turn to 236.**
- *If 7-12,* **turn to 385.**

273

You notice the little table that McDonald mentioned lying on its side by the far easy chair. **Turn to 259.**

274

"I wish you knew more about it," you say casually. "Do you know anyone who might know the secrets of this place?"

Grant smiles a little. "Well, I cannot be certain," he says, "so I'm only guessing, you understand."

"I understand," you answer quickly. "I of course will be discreet, if there is any need to confirm your guess."

"Well," Sir George goes on. "You may or may not know it, but two of our members, the Earl of Waynesborough and his son Lord Grayson, gave this house to the club, shortly after the club was founded. It was their family townhouse for years, but they found it too expensive to maintain. Neither of them was here last night—they are having a very nice affair for all the members at their country place in Kent." ***Check Deduction 7. Turn to 333.***

275
You wonder what secrets the billiard room might hide.
- *If you checked Clue B,* **turn to 276.**
- *Otherwise,* **turn to 459.**

276
You remember that McDonald did not search the room for secret exits. You wonder whether you should—a secret exit might go a long way toward clearing Watson's name.
- *If you search for an exit,* **turn to 307.**
- *Otherwise,* **turn to 422.**

277
You decide that a man could possibly have escaped the billiard room by the trapdoor, slipped out of the office, and then mingled with the members. **Turn to 282.**

278
Strickland glances at his list, but obviously has already made his decision. "The next man you should talk to is Thomas Sullivan," he tells you. "He was playing chess with Sir George when the murder was discovered by Chambers."
- *If you want to talk to Sullivan,* **turn to 203.**
- *Otherwise,* **turn to 513.**

279
"When I was at Baker Street this morning," you begin, "I was very surprised at the condition of the rooms. I had thought to have a difficult time sorting through your brother's property, but instead I found the rooms ready for your brother to move back in today. Why have you gone to so much trouble?"

Mycroft looks troubled at the question. Finally he says, "I am not certain. Most of it arises from my eccentric nature, combined with the pain of Sherlock's death. Maintaining his home helps me pretend that nothing has changed in the well-ordered course of my life." **Turn to 504.**

280

You search the desk for hollow legs or secret compartments and find nothing of any use. Reluctantly, you admit that you have done all you can here and send for the police. **Turn to 391.**

281

You try to think of how you would hide in the billiard room. Looking around the room you wonder whether a man could hide successfully behind the floor-length window curtains.

- *If you ask Strickland to hide,* **turn to 474.**
- *Otherwise,* **turn to 350.**

282

Strickland is obviously very impatient with you. You wonder whether you should look over the billiard room again or begin to interview the witnesses who were in the club the night of the killing.

- *If you look over the room again,* **turn to 284.**
- *Otherwise,* **turn to 558.**

283

You have found nothing of use in your search. You prepare to leave, and with a start you realize that you've been here more than two hours. You had better get away quickly, as Marshall might return at any moment!

- *If you leave immediately,* **turn to 365.**
- *If you take the time to arrange everything as it was when you arrived,* **turn to 344.**

284

"I need to go over the room again," you tell the chairman, and he reluctantly goes back upstairs with you. The constable lets you back into the billiard room, though he looks rather surprised. *Check Deduction 5.* **Turn to 281.**

"May I ask you a few questions first, Mr. Strickland?" you ask. "It may help me understand the sequence of events."

Strickland looks surprised, then agrees. "Very well, though I do not know anything else."

- *If you ask him to describe what happened,* **turn to 534.**
- *Otherwise,* **turn to 207.**

286

At a word from Strickland, a servant summons Sir George Grant. He is a short stout man, with a halo of fluffy white hair circling a bald head. You wonder how much he noticed that night. He looks like a man who doesn't pay much attention to things around him."

"Good evening, sir," he says very politely. "I understand you are looking into the unfortunate affair of yesterday evening."

"I am, Sir George," you reply, offering him a chair with a wave of your hand. "I very much appreciate your cooperation. Could you tell me exactly what happened, and what you saw last night?"

"Certainly," Grant replies. "When Chambers called out, I was playing chess in the room just across the hall, playing with Mr. Sullivan. With Chambers yelling 'Murder! Murder!' at the top of his lungs, we both jumped up and ran out in the hall. Chambers led us back in there and we found poor Terry Milton lying behind the billiard table. John Watson ran in just behind us, and being a doctor he bent over to confirm what we all could see, that Milton was dead."

- *If you ask him how Watson behaved,* **turn to 211.**
- *If you do not ask him any more questions,* **turn to 333.**
- *Otherwise,* **turn to 132.**

287

The trellis that supports the ivy seems to provide an easy ladder for you, but as you pull yourself up, you hear a voice yell: "Stop thief! Police! Police!" Turning your head you see a man leaning from a window in the neighboring house. Hurriedly you drop to the ground, circle the house and jump the back wall. You are happy to slip away without encountering a bobbie. **Turn to 560.**

288

You look over the body, trying not to disturb the evidence. You find no indication of murder and then try to decide what to do next.

- *If you send immediately for the police,* **turn to 391.**
- *If you search the office,* **turn to 428.**

289

"I would like you to think about the billiard room, when you entered it," you say. "Was any of the furniture knocked over?"

"Furniture?" Lord Howard almost explodes, "How would you expect me to know anything about furniture when a man I've known for ten years is lying there dead. Don't be such a bloody fool!" It takes you an uncomfortable moment to recover from the Lord's outburst. **Turn to 508.**

290

"Now, when Chambers discovered the body and screamed for help, you ran upstairs to the billiard room," you say, looking at Marshall, and he nods. "What did you see when you entered the room? Think carefully, please; any detail might be crucial to the investigation."

Taking your request to heart, Marshall pauses for a few seconds before speaking. Then he says: "The most striking thing of course, was the body, sprawled on the floor over behind the billiard table. I knew it must be Sir Terrence from the clothes. Watson was kneeling beside him, and telling everyone to stay back, so that we wouldn't trample on any possible clues."

"Do you remember who was there when you entered?' you continue.

"I'm not certain," he answers, "there was such a lot of shouting and moving about. Grant was there, and Sullivan, but I can't recall if any other members were in the room before I came in. Then Watson told us Sir Terrence was dead, and Strickland here sent for the police immediately. That's all I can remember."

- *If you checked Clue C,* **turn to 527.**
- *If you are done questioning him,* **turn to 405.**
- *Otherwise,* **turn to 334.**

291

As Watson guiltily shuffles his feet, doubt stirs in your heart. **Turn to 592.**

292

The racing hansom leaves you far behind. Winded, you can do nothing but sigh in frustration. **Turn to 594.**

293

You try to think through all you know of Marshall's connection to the case and how suspicious his actions appear to be. You wonder: dare I search his house to uncover further evidence?

- *If you search his house,* **turn to 470.**
- *Otherwise,* **turn to 560.**

294

"When you saw Dr. Watson, how did he behave?" you ask.

"Behave, sir?" he answers, clearly puzzled. "What do you mean by how he behaved, sir?" **Pick a number** *and add your Communication bonus:*

- *If 2-7,* **turn to 408.**
- *If 8-12,* **turn to 296.**

295

You wonder if he knows anything you haven't heard about the fight between Watson and Sir Terrence.

- *If you ask about the fight,* **turn to 411.**
- *If you are through questioning Lord Howard,*
    turn to 561.

- *Otherwise,* **turn to 130.**

296

"When Dr. Watson left the billiard room, did he seem upset?" you ask, trying to overcome Chambers' obvious confusion.

Chambers thinks a moment, then shakes his head as he says, "No sir, he didn't act queer at all. He just acted like he always does, nodded a little polite like and went on his way downstairs. Course I don't pay much mind to the members sir. It's not my place to." **Turn to 370.**

297

You look straight at Marshall, hardening your face to show your displeasure with him. He does not turn a hair. "Mr. Marshall," you begin, "I know that you are a friend of Dr. Watson, and I am certain you want to help solve this mystery, so I cannot understand why you have not told me the complete truth about this case." Marshall pales a little at your words. **Pick a number** *and add your Communication bonus:*

- *If 2-9,* **turn to 355.**
- *If 10-12,* **turn to 392.**

298

"In the billiard room, over near the windows, there was a little table knocked over," you say to Sullivan. "Did you happen to notice it when you came into the room, or did someone bump into it later?"

Sullivan sits very still and concentrates for a minute or two, as though mentally cataloging every object in the room at the moment he entered it. "You mean the little table by the easy chair nearest the windows?" he asks, and you nod. "That was knocked over when I came in," he says firmly. "I wondered what had happened to it. Chambers wouldn't have come near it when he ran out of the room and neither Grant nor I touched it when we ran in. But it was knocked over when I entered the room."

"Do you have any idea what could have happened to it?" you ask.

"Well, I just thought of one," he answers, "though my idea is rather far-fetched. If someone killed Sir Terrence before Watson came into the room, and hid behind the drapes while Watson was sitting there, he might have run across the room to hide behind the door when Chambers ran out into the hall and screamed for help. Then the killer either mingled with the rest of us or slipped out into the hall when we were all looking down at the body." *Check Clue L.* **Turn to 455.**

299

"Do you remember whom you were talking to downstairs?" you ask. "That is, who was there when Chambers sounded the alarm?"

"I remember precisely sir," Howard answers. "I was talking with Lord Howard and with Edward Lawrence. Lewis and Martin had been with us, but they both had engagements and left the club before we learned of the murder. The three of us ran up the stairs together, and I was the first one into the billiard room." *Check Clue O.* **Turn to 190.**

300

Locke listens to your explanation, then nods. "That is sufficient proof, I think," he says. "The man was not where he says he was. When a man with no alibi lies to you, it certainly suggests that he could have been there to do it. And no one mentions his running into the billiard room — he could have been hidden and mingled with the others as they streamed in." **Turn to 318.**

"Now, try to be precise if you can," you continue, "and tell me exactly what you were doing when you heard of the murder, and what you saw when you went upstairs?"

"I was with Johnson in the supper room when Chambers called out," Strickland says. "We were checking that everything was set up properly for the late supper—we always put a light meal out around eleven, as many of the members keep odd hours. With Chambers screaming, 'Help, murder!' at the top of his lungs, we ran upstairs and into the billiard room, but we were about the last men to arrive. The other members were clustered by the billiard table looking down at the body. Watson was kneeling by the body, and after confirming that Sir Terrence was dead, he told the others to keep back and not to touch anything."

"And all the members were there? None came in after you?" you ask.

"Yes, I looked around to check, once I was certain we had a murder to deal with, and I saw them all. I am sure no one came in after Johnson and I ran in."

- *If you have no more questions for Strickland,*
  turn to 228.
- *If you checked Clue C,* **turn to 457.**
- *Otherwise,* **turn to 207.**

302

"When I searched the billiard room," you begin, "I found that there was a trapdoor under the table. Did you know that there was such a thing in this house?"

"A trapdoor?" he answers. "My word, how bizarre! You mean there really is such a thing in this dear old place? Well, that's often the way with these old houses." **Pick a number** *and add your Intuition bonus:*

- *If 2-7,* **turn to 333.**
- *If 8-12,* **turn to 367.**

303

"I hate to say what I have to say," you announce, "for it is not the solution that you gentlemen wanted, but I am forced to conclude that Dr. Watson killed Sir Terrence. The evidence pointing to him is too strong. He probably met Sir Terrence in the billiard room by mischance, and their argument resumed. Finally, provoked beyond bearing, Watson grabbed the poker and smashed in Sir Terrence's head."

The three men stare at you in open-mouthed astonishment. It is finally Captain Locke who answers. "Nonsense!" he snaps in an outraged tone that makes you flinch. "If Watson murdered a man, he would not sit in the room for thirty minutes confronting his dirty work. He would rather hastily get away, and hope no one saw him. The man who committed this crime planned it and slipped up behind Sir Terrence. If the killer, in the course of an argument, had grabbed the poker and run across the room with it, he would not have been able to hit Sir Terrence in the back of his head." **Turn to 525.**

304

"When I was in the billiard room," you say, "I noticed that a little table near the windows was knocked over. Did you notice whether it was knocked down, sir? You seem to be an observant man."

"The little table by the armchair?" he asks, and you nod. "Yes, I saw it sir. It was knocked over when I got there. Thomas Sullivan was standing near it, and I think he must have knocked it over himself. Dr. Watson was kneeling by the body, and kept telling us to stay back, so we wouldn't spoil any evidence. Not that there's anybody in London who can find that kind of evidence, now that Sherlock Holmes is dead. I kept a close eye on Watson and the body from then on."

"Did you see any sign of him destroying anything?" you ask.

"Well, no, he just confirmed that Sir Terrence was dead. Then someone else asked how long he had been dead and Watson said a few minutes at least, though he couldn't be very exact."

"And was anything else said then?" you continue.

"Well, Watson acted very puzzled, and said he had been in

that room himself for the past half hour. He seemed shocked at the idea that he had sat in the same room with a dead man for half an hour and not known it. Or maybe he was shocked he had the nerve to stay there that long after he killed the man."
Turn to 190.

305

You run over the evidence in your mind, and try to decide what Captain Lawrence might know.

- *If you ask what happened before the murder,* **turn to 381.**
- *If you have nothing further to ask him,* **turn to 436.**
- *If you pause for a moment to decide,* **turn to 101.**

306

Strickland heaves a deep sigh of relief, glances at his list to confirm something, then smiles at you. "You will be pleased to know," he says, "that only one more witness remains to be interviewed."

"Who is that?" you ask, standing and stretching to get rid of some stiffness.

"Christopher Marshall, a very good friend of Dr. Watson," Strickland answers. "He was in the game of whist, as you know. When Johnson brought us our light meal, he told me that Marshall had just arrived at the club. He had some business at the government offices that couldn't wait."

You wonder if you will learn anything of use from Marshall, or whether it will waste time to talk to him.

- *If you talk to Marshall,* **turn to 369.**
- *Otherwise,* **turn to 143.**

307

With a quick word of explanation to the chairman, you begin to search for a possible secret exit from the room. He is obviously impatient, but you do not let that distract you. A quick examination of the walls show that they cannot possibly hide a secret exit, and you begin to examine the floor with all possible care.

- *If you search the floor further,* **turn to 212.**
- *If you decide not to search,* **turn to 422.**

308

You wonder if Marshall noticed anything the other witnesses missed when he entered the billiard room after the murder.

- *If you ask him,* **turn to 290.**
- *Otherwise,* **turn to 310.**

309

You slip quietly up the stairs, hoping that your quarry has no chance to see or hear you. You wait until you hear an office door open and close before walking down the hall to listen from outside.

The two men begin talking quietly, but soon the conversation grows vehement. You recognize that Marshall is one of the men, and that the other is Symington. You understand enough of what they say to be certain that the two men are partners. Symington's voice blurs, as though he had turned away from you, and you lean closer to the door, hoping to hear more. *Check Clue T.* **Pick a number** *and add your Observation bonus:*

- *If 2-7,* **turn to 105.**
- *If 8-12,* **turn to 401.**

310

You realize that you have learned most of the information Marshall can tell you, and you wrack your brain to see if you've missed any relevant questions. You wonder vaguely what opinion he held of Sir Terrence.

- *If you ask his opinion,* **turn to 346.**
- *Otherwise,* **turn to 405.**

311

Though you have asked him everything you want to learn from him, Lewis continues to chat with you for a few minutes more, tossing around various wild ideas of how the murder occurred. Finally, amid a cheerful exchange of compliments, you thank him for his help and he leaves. **Turn to 306.**

312

"You say you wanted to stir the fire," you say carefully. Chambers nods. "Was the room chilly when you came in? Would Dr. Watson have wished to stir up the fire?"

Chambers shakes his head. "No sir, the room was nicely warm. It's just that the logs was breaking up, so that if I hadn't taken care of it, it would have been a little chilly before long. And the members don't bother themselves much with the fires anyway—even if they do start to feel cold. They yell for one of us to take care of it rather than doing it themselves." He glances at Strickland and hurriedly adds, "Of course, that's as things should be, sir. We're paid to keep things comfy for the members." **Turn to 150.**

313

Locke listens carefully to your explanation, looks at Mycroft, and they both nod. "Very good," Mycroft says. "You have established a strong connection between Sir Terrence and Mr. Marshall. A man might well kill to hide such behaviour, especially with reports that Sir Terrence was about to be investigated."

- *If you checked Clue S,* **turn to 372.**
- *Otherwise,* **turn to 195.**

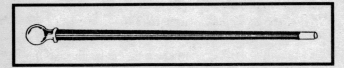

314

"Did you see Dr. Watson when he came into the room?" you ask Sullivan.

"See him?" he answers, "Well I didn't see him come through the door, but he must have come right behind us. As he is a physician, we let him look at Sir Terrence, and confirm what we knew with half an eye—that Milton was dead as a door-nail."

"And how did Watson behave?" you continue.

"He was very calm, given the circumstances," Sullivan replies, "but then he wouldn't have worked with Sherlock Holmes if he wasn't a cool hand. Some of the men actually thought Watson could be the killer, if you can imagine that."

Pick a number *and add your Observation bonus:*

- *If 2-6,* **turn to 337.**
- *If 7-12,* **turn to 538.**

315

You have finished your investigation at Symington's office. After taking a minute or two to order the new evidence in your mind, you consider your next step.

- *If you checked Decision 23,* **turn to 349.**
- *Otherwise,* **turn to 107.**

316

After a few minutes, one of the shopkeepers comes up with a bobbie and asks why you are loitering in his neighborhood. You show the bobbie your note from McDonald, but while you're settling this matter the visitor comes down and walks up the street. He has a good start on you by the time you are free to follow him.

- *If you follow the visitor,* **turn to 174.**
- *If you go up to see Symington,* **turn to 265.**
- *If you decide you've wasted enough time around this area,* **turn to 518.**

317

With a mighty splash, accompanied by the laughter of the launch's crew, you land in the water. Desperately you try to swim back to the shore. **Pick a number** *and add your Athletics bonus:*

- *If 2-4,* **turn to 131.**
- *If 5-12,* **turn to 491.**

318

"Now that we have covered method and opportunity," Locke says, "we are left with the key factor: motive. Why would Marshall wish to kill Sir Terrence?"

- *If you checked Clue X or Deduction 27,* **turn to 313.**
- *If you checked Clue E or Deduction 8 and also checked Deduction 4,* **turn to 254.**
- *Otherwise,* **turn to 180.**

319

"Did you know that there was a trapdoor in the floor of the billiard room?" you ask Sullivan. "Under the table, in fact."

"A trapdoor?" he answers, "You don't say so. What an odd thing. I never imagined that there was such a thing in this place."

"Do you have any idea who might have known?" you continue.

"No, I don't. It's a fairly old house after all." **Turn to 448.**

"Now, Chambers," you say, "when you went into the room, did you notice anything out of place in the room, anything besides the dead man, of course?"

Chambers shakes his head and asks, "What sort of things sir. Did someone else say something was out of place?"

"What I'm thinking of," you continue, "is the little table near the windows, the one beside the easy chair. Was it knocked down when you entered?"

Chambers shakes his head. "I don't know sir, I don't remember." You wonder how to get an answer from him.

- *If you decide he doesn't know,* **turn to 439.**
- *If you urge him to think harder,* **turn to 379.**
- *If you try to find of a better way to ask him,* **turn to 194.**

"You say the evidence will force you to arrest him," you say slowly. "Do you believe that Watson committed this crime, Mr. McDonald?"

McDonald shakes his head. "That's another reason why I haven't arrested him. I know the man, and I cannot conceive of him committing murder. I especially cannot conceive of him killing a man and then sitting in the room for half an hour with the body growing cold. If Sir Terrence provoked or threatened him, Watson might have killed the fellow, but he would not have hit him over the back of the head with a poker."

"Then why arrest him at all?" you reply.

"Because I am bound by law and evidence," McDonald answers, "and the evidence points so squarely to Dr. Watson that in good conscience I could do nought else. Nor would my superiors permit it. Mr. Lestrade accompanied me to the scene when we first heard of the murder," he adds, "but as soon as we heard the outline of the evidence he had to go home. Lestrade's lumbago flared up so that the poor man could hardly move. But I understood, of course. Lestrade has been a friend of Dr. Watson for many years. With the circumstantial evidence so damning to Watson, Lestrade's lumbago saved him from being forced to arrest his old friend." **Turn to 152.**

322

You search Symington's office carefully. Finally, when you are about to give up, you leaf through the books behind his desk. A slip of paper falls out of one of them. You pick it up, look at it, and stare in astonishment. It is a very odd piece of work:

217	38	46	117	29	38	home
12	2	202	146	88	199	300
top	194	105	77	high	200	64

You look at the little note, wondering what it means.

- *If you checked Clue I,* **turn to 360.**
- *Otherwise,* **turn to 409.**

323

You climb the basement steps to the ground floor, and look around. The rooms here are what you would expect: parlour, dining room, sitting room and kitchen. None of them looks like a place where Marshall would keep his papers.

A little nervous about your chances of escape, you go up to the next floor. There you find two bedrooms and a small study, which Marshall obviously uses as an office. You search it as expeditiously as possible, but find nothing but the most ordinary sorts of letters and business papers. **Pick a number** *and add your Observation bonus:*

- *If 2-7,* **turn to 283.**
- *If 8-12,* **turn to 571.**

324

"Did you know there was a trapdoor under the billiard table?" you ask.

He looks surprised at you, then laughs. "You have done your homework, sir," he laughs, "though I think it was a waste of your time. That trap only leads into the Club Secretary's office, and no man trying to hide could safely come out of that room. He wouldn't know if there was anyone in the hall, because the office has a solid door."

Strickland stares at Lawrence in shock, and demands, "Edward, how did you know of that trapdoor? I didn't learn of it myself until tonight."

The captain laughs a self-satisfied laugh. "Lord Grayson told me," he explains, "one night when he was drunk. He had an idea that we might play a joke on the secretary, but we decided it was too much trouble." ***Check Deduction 5 and Deduction 7***. **Turn to 436.**

325

You explain the connection between the two clues. "You see, gentlemen," you say, "as Chambers was certain that no table was knocked over, and Mr. Sullivan will swear that it was lying down when he entered the room, someone must have knocked it over between the moment Chambers ran out of the room and the time he returned with Sullivan and Grant."

"Aye," Mycroft replies, "that's very true. It seems obvious that the man who knocked the table over hid afterward — perhaps behind the door. And a man who behaved in that way almost certainly was the murderer. I think this proves, Inspector, that Watson did not kill Sir Terrence." ***Check Decision 10***. **Turn to 404.**

326

You cannot find any sign of a trapdoor in the billiard room floor. You wonder if you missed some key sign of a hidden exit, but you've spent all the time you can afford on the search. **Turn to 127.**

327

"Did you know there was a trapdoor hidden in the billiard room floor?" you ask.

"A trapdoor, no, I didn't know anything about a trapdoor," he answers. "I must admit that it doesn't surprise me much," he adds. "These old houses are loaded with all sorts of hidden passages. Very useful they were, to householders who kept mistresses, or needed to hide from the law. Now, the members who would be most likely to know about that trapdoor would be Lord Grayson, and his father, the Earl of Waynesborough. The Earl gave the house to the club, when it became too expensive for him to maintain. But of course, neither of them was within forty miles of here last night." ***Check Deduction 7.*** **Turn to 129.**

328

You think about the trapdoor in the billiard room floor and wonder if Lord Howard knows anything about it.

- *If you ask him about the trapdoor,* **turn to 142.**
- *Otherwise,* **turn to 561.**

329

On the street corner you see an organ grinder. Might he have seen something odd that night? **Turn to 595.**

330

Strickland brings in Edwin Johnson, the club's butler. Johnson is a tall thin man, with a very calm, dignified face. He is obviously the soul of discretion.

- *If you ask him if he heard of the fight,* **turn to 167.**
- *Otherwise,* **turn to 397.**

331

There is a clipping on Waynesborough, discussing a murder that may have involved the Earl. According to the story, a footman who had made advances to the Earl's cousin had been found drowned in a pond on the Earl's property. It was unclear whether the death was an accident or murder, and it had never come to trial. Holmes' notes mention that the Earl is known to be bad-tempered and also describe him as a perfect mark for unsrupulous entrepreneurs. **Turn to 465.**

332

Your curiosity spurred by Watson's careful comments about Sir Terrence, you wonder what he really felt about the dead man.

- *If you ask his opinion of Sir Terrence,* **turn to 256.**
- *Otherwise,* **turn to 361.**

333

Feeling that you have learned all you can from Sir George, you thank him for his help and watch thoughtfully as he leaves the room. **Turn to 278.**

334

You wonder if Marshall knew about the trap door in the billiard room.

- *If you ask him about it,* **turn to 416.**
- *If you are finished questioning him,* **turn to 405.**
- *Otherwise,* **turn to 310.**

335

"What were you doing when you heard the servant call out?" you ask Lawrence.

The captain hardly pauses to think. "Oh, I was downstairs, sir," he answers. "I was talking to some of the other members, when we heard the man yelling. Naturally we all ran upstairs. In the billiard room we found Dr. Watson kneeling over the body, with some other men watching him, but even at ten feet I could see Sir Terrence was dead. From then on I kept an eye on my fellow members, to see if anyone acted oddly. I'm afraid I didn't pay much attention to the scene of the crime, though."

- *If you ask who he was talking to downstairs,* **turn to 217.**
- *Otherwise,* **turn to 569.**

336

"I don't see any use in going through this trapdoor," you tell the chairman. "I doubt that anyone could escape in this fashion."

"I'm pleased you are not wasting the time," he answers. "The murderer could not have safely exited the room below this one, anyway."

You notice the floor-length curtains in front of the windows and wonder if someone could hide behind them.

- *If you ask the chairman to hide,* **turn to 474.**
- *Otherwise,* **turn to 350.**

337

You try to think of other areas where Sullivan might know something useful.

- *If you checked Clue C,* **turn to 521.**
- *If you do not wish to ask more questions,* **turn to 448.**
- *If you need time to decide what to ask next* **turn to 455.**

338

Two growlers take you, McDonald, and four constables to a street a block away from Marshall's house. Quickly, the Inspector gives his instructions. "Moore and Lee," he tells two constables, "Go to the front door and knock loudly, shouting for him to come out. He will probably try to run out the back. I will be waiting there with Andrews. Reynolds," he adds, pointing to his last constable, "take your station on the northeast corner of the lot, so that you can see him if he somehow slips out the front, or the east side. You, sir," he says to you, "should watch the back and west side. Now gentlemen, let us all carry out our duties well, and we will take the villain."

- *If you checked Decision 26,* **turn to 198.**
- *If you have checked Clue Y, but not Decision 26,*
    turn to 492.
- *If you checked neither Decision 26 nor Clue Y,*
    turn to 388.

339

"Inspector McDonald," you say, and he looks back towards you, "if the evidence is so formidable against Dr. Watson, why haven't you arrested him?"

The policeman looks embarrassed. "Well sir," he answers, "It may be a dereliction of my duty, but I have a difficult time arresting a man I like. I convinced my superiors that I should wait a little while, to be thoroughly convinced by the evidence, as an arrest would be so damaging to a man of his position. I cannot delay long, however. If you can't give me good cause to doubt my conclusions by tonight, I shall arrest Dr. Watson tomorrow." **Pick a number** *and add your Intuition bonus:*

- *If 2-5,* **turn to 152.**
- *If 6-12,* **turn to 321.**

340

"Did you hear," you say to Martin, "that when Mr. Strickland and I searched the billiard room, we found a trapdoor in the floor? Did you know there was such a thing in this building?"

"A trapdoor?" he answers, clearly surprised. "Who would have guessed? No, I never heard any such stories about the old club. I'll tell you who would know about it, though. The Earl of Waynesborough gave the house to the club, and his son Lord Grayson is also a member. They'd both be very likely to

341

You and McDonald agree that you have completed your search and leave Symington's office. When McDonald's cab drops you at your rooms, you agree that you will meet at Mycroft's the next evening to summarize the case, and prepare to make the arrest of the killer, if you have discovered his identity. **Turn to 475.**

342

Your patience is rewarded. The visitor comes down from Symington's office and strides briskly up the street. As he turns you get a good look at him. With a start you realize that it is Watson's friend, Christopher Marshall. *Check Clue T*.

- *If you go up to see Symington,* **turn to 265.**
- *If you follow Marshall,* **turn to 149.**

343

It occurs to you that this man might very well want to help you find a crucial piece of evidence in Sir Terrence's papers, if such a document exists.

"Would you help me go through his papers?" you ask Perkins. "Your familiarity with your master's business and habits might make the difference in catching the killer or missing an incriminating document." **Pick a number** *and add your Communication bonus:*

- *If 2-4,* **turn to 523.**
- *If 5-12,* **turn to 581.**

344

While you would not like Marshall to catch you in his house, you decide that it would be worse to leave evidence of your visit. You carefully put everything away and straighten the furniture. Then you hurry downstairs, slip out the back door, and finally swing over the rear wall. As you get your feet under you, you hear a cab rattle up in front of the house and stop. You have left just in time! **Turn to 560.**

345

The pleasant weather makes you feel so good that you are somehow certain that you will find the key evidence today.

- *If you checked Deduction 14,* **turn to 123.**
- *Otherwise,* **turn to 107.**

346

"You knew Sir Terrence, of course," you begin, glancing at Marshall. "Could you tell me what you thought of the man? Knowing more about him might help explain why he was killed."

"Of course, of course," Marshall answers, "I quite agree. Sir Terrence was a fairly decent chap, though he could have an uncivil tongue in his head. There were stories that he toyed with other men's wives, though I don't know if anyone ever proved that. And of course, his business failures made him unpopular."

"Was he a poor businessman?" you ask.

"Most would say so," Marshall answers, "and as he had three companies fail in the last decade, I would have to agree with them. If he wasn't a poor businessman, he was a dishonest one. Of course, he always tried high-risk, gambling ventures, so his failures may have been the result of bad luck."

"Did you ever invest with him?"

"Oh no," Marshall answers, laughing and shaking his head. "No, if I want to gamble, I stick to cards or horses. I wouldn't have recommended Marshall's operations to anyone as an investment."

- *If you checked Clue E or Deduction 8,* **turn to 446.**
- *Otherwise,* **turn to 405.**

347

You consider further questions for Lewis, wondering if he knows anything of use.

- *If you ask his opinion of Sir Terrence,* **turn to 358.**
- *If you are finished questioning him,* **turn to 311.**
- *Otherwise,* **turn to 246.**

Satisfied that you have examined everything necessary, you prepare to leave Marshall's house. You are a little startled to realize that you have spent more than two hours here. The sooner you leave, the better. You look at the disarranged room and wonder if you should risk taking the time to tidy it. You will have a good deal of explaining to do if you are caught in someone else's house.

- *If you straighten the room before you leave,* **turn to 344.**
- *Otherwise,* **turn to 365.**

349

You recall that you have permission to look at Sherlock Holmes' papers and records in his former lodgings in Baker Street. Might you find something useful there?

- *If you go to Baker Street,* **turn to 136.**
- *Otherwise,* **turn to 107.**

350

You decide that Strickland is already so irritated that it would be unwise to ask him to do anything that might upset him even more. **Turn to 583.**

351

You think hard, trying to decide if there is anything else that Sir George might be able to tell you.

- *If you checked Clue G,* **turn to 528.**
- *Otherwise,* **turn to 333.**

352

"I think it would be best to talk to Johnson, the butler," Strickland says, "if you want to see him. I know he was downstairs from eight-thirty until after the body was discovered."

- *If you want to talk to Johnson,* **turn to 330.**
- *Otherwise,* **turn to 447.**

353

Finished examining Symington's body, you rise and look around. You wonder if there are any secrets hidden in this room; information that might help you solve the Milton murder.

- *If you search the room,* **turn to 434.**
- *If you leave,* **turn to 341.**
- *Otherwise,* **turn to 440.**

354

"What do we know of the Earl?" you ask. "What kind of a man is he?"

"The Earl," McDonald ponders, "I met the Earl when we investigated a robbery at his house. He is a bluff, hearty man, but also the sort who is very bitter toward any person who does him wrong. When I discovered that one of his servants was the thief, it took two men to keep him from beating the poor bugger to a pulp. There have been other stories to suggest he has a high temper."

- *If you checked Deduction 7,* **turn to 376.**
- *Otherwise,* **turn to 471.**

355

The paleness in Marshall's face is replaced by an angry red shade, and he rises suddenly and steps towards you. With an almost visible effort of will he stops, shakes his fist at you, then turns and stomps from the room. As he leaves he shouts: "I see no use in wasting time with a man who does not have sense enough to tell a lie from the truth, and who treats an ally like a criminal! If you ever speak to me again, sir, I shall give you a good caning!"

Strickland looks at you, then shakes his head, his disgust obvious. **Turn to 143.**

Chambers is a short, slender man, with a thin face and sandy hair. He is obviously nervous as he stands in front of you, shifting from one foot to the other. "Sit down and make yourself comfortable," you say softly. "You have nothing to worry about, Chambers. No one suspects you of doing anything wrong."

Chambers perches on the edge of one of the chairs, and says very softly: "Thank you, sir. The police were so angry with me last night that I was proper scared when Mr. Strickland told me I had to talk to another bloke about it. And it was proper horrible, sir, to find the poor man like that."

"I understand," you tell him. "Now I'd appreciate it if you'd tell me exactly why you were upstairs when you found Sir Terrence."

"Oh, that's where I'm supposed to be," he says hurriedly. "There's a lavatory and a couple of small rooms the members use up there, and one of us stays up there every night to see that everything is just like it should be — dirty dishes taken away and the fires kept going and that sort of thing sir."

- *If you ask him about seeing Watson,* **turn to 398.**
- *If you don't want to ask any more questions,* **turn to 439.**
- *Otherwise,* **turn to 370.**

You decide that you had better see Sir Terrence's rival, Symington, immediately. He may hold the key to the entire investigation. ***Check Decision 23.*** **Turn to 103.**

"You had known Sir Terrence for some time, hadn't you?" you ask, and Lewis nods. "Would you tell me your opinion of him, please," you continue. "What sort of man was he?"

"I guess I can say something," he says, obviously reluctant. "You won't think badly of me, if it doesn't sound right, I hope. I have no intention of speaking ill of the dead, but it may come out sounding that way."

"I understand," you say, and Strickland hurriedly echoes you.

"Very well," Lewis continues, "I wanted to be certain of that, because I'm not at all sure that my opinion does the man justice. You see, I lost rather a large amount of money in two of his companies, and I do think a man shouldn't go into business unless he knows what he's doing. And I had heard definitely that both companies had excellent potential. They were opportunities which could hardly go wrong. So I put quite a lot into the ventures and lost virtually all of my investment." **Pick a number** *and add your Intuition bonus:*

- *If 2-6,* **turn to 246.**
- *If 7-12,* **turn to 374.**

359

"Can you tell me what happened last night?" you ask.

"Certainly," he answers, "though I told McDonald everything I knew. Last night I went to a club, "The Three Continents", for supper and a game of whist. My partner Marshall and I played perfectly in the last hand, and made a slam to win the rubber. Well, Sir Terrence made a fuss over the matter, though his losses were less than a pound, and accused me of cheating. We insulted each other for a while. Finally I tired of the fellow and laid him out with a punch between the eyes."

"What did you do then?" you ask. "Did you stay in the card room or go elsewhere?"

"Oh, my friend Marshall hustled me out of the room," he answers. "He didn't want any more trouble, even though the club is free about such matters. He led me to a parlor, where one of the servants got me a glass of brandy. Then I went up to the small billiard room, to drink it in peace."

"When did you do that?" you ask.

"I really don't know," he answers. "I didn't pay attention to the clock. I sat and read for a while, while I drank my brandy. When I finished I went downstairs, but before I'd gotten to the foot of the stair, one of the servants started screaming. I ran back up and into the room I'd just left. I was just behind some of the other members. Sir Terrence was lying in the corner, behind the billiard table. Someone had smashed his head with the poker from the fireplace."

"Could you tell how long he'd been dead?"

"Well, I did not perform an autopsy," Watson answers testily, "but he had been dead for a few minutes at least. He must have been dead and lying there when I entered the room. It was odd because I saw no one leave as I went upstairs and down the hall to the room."

- *If you checked Clue C,* **turn to 210.**
- *Otherwise,* **turn to 332.**

360

You look at the odd note and realize that it's in the same code as the note you found in the billiard room. However, you have absolutely no way to ascertain what book or paper is keyed to this note, and you do not have time to experiment. You put the note away in your pocket and try to decide what to do next. There might be something useful hidden in Symington's desk, but at the same time you know you should report his death to the police as soon as possible. ***Check Clue R.***

- *If you call the police,* **turn to 391.**
- *If you search the desk,* **turn to 225.**

361

You remember that Sir Terrence had mentioned Watson's relations with some woman in their argument.

- *If you ask Watson about this argument,* **turn to 224.**
- *Otherwise,* **turn to 232.**

362

Though Marshall tells this story very glibly, you realize that he is lying to you. Something in the way he tells it does not ring true.

- *If you demand an explanation for the lie,* **turn to 297.**
- *Otherwise,* **turn to 308.**

363

You stand about half a block from the building where Symington has his office. Traffic keeps you from riding closer. You pause for just a moment — you want to be certain about what to ask him.

- *If you checked Decision 22,* **turn to 265.**
- *Otherwise,* **turn to 506.**

364

Realizing that the club was once a private house, you wonder whether there might be a secret exit somewhere in it. Such an exit might help to clear Watson.

- *If you search for it,* **turn to 307.**
- *If you decide not to,* **turn to 422.**

365

Worried about the time, you run down the stairs, open the kitchen door and slip out the back. As you vault the back fence, you here the clatter of hoofs on the pavement, a noise that stops in front of the house. You quietly slip off through the dark streets. *Check Decision 26.* **Turn to 560.**

366

You eat a quick supper and try to decide what you want to do the next day. What information will give you the best chance to learn something conclusive? **Turn to 242.**

367

While Grant obviously doesn't know anything about the trapdoor, you wonder whether he can tell you who does know the secrets of the house.

- *If you ask him who might know,* **turn to 274.**
- *Otherwise,* **turn to 333.**

368

"Did you know that there was a trapdoor in the billiard room?" you ask, making a last effort at learning something from Captain Lawrence.

"And what difference would that make?" he answers with

his usual sharpness. "It leads to the secretary's office, and no one could safely get away by that route. He wouldn't know whether there was anyone in the hall when he exited the office."

"How did you know about the trapdoor?" Strickland asks, shocked.

"Oh, Lord Grayson told me about it one night, when he'd had a little too much to drink," Lawrence answers. "He suggested we play a trick on the secretary, but it didn't seem worth the effort." *Check Deduction 5 and Deduction 7.* **Turn to 436.**

369

Marshall comes into the room. He is a man of medium height, but built very powerfully, with huge, strong hands. The impression of raw power is moderated, however, by his warm smile. You remember that he was in the whist game with Watson and Sir Terrence, and wonder what he will tell you about the fight.

- *If you ask him about the fight,* **turn to 548.**
- *Otherwise,* **turn to 112.**

370

"Now, Chambers," you say, "just relax and think carefully. Then tell me what you saw when you found the body."

Chambers relaxes and begins the story he's obviously told several times already. "I went in there, sir, and began to tidy up the things that needed to be tidied. I was going to stir the fire but the poker weren't there. Then I saw something else over by the billiard table, and I ran over there and saw poor Sir Terrence lying on his face. The back of his head was a proper mess sir, and the poker was lying by him all bloody. Well, when I sees that I done like any man would, I run out in the hall yelling for help. Thank God, the other gentlemen come quick and took matters in hand." **Pick a number** *and add your Intuition bonus:*

- *If 2-7,* **turn to 150.**
- *If 8-12,* **turn to 450.**

371

"They must be sort of careless jokers, if you can see the signs from the outside," you comment.

"No, no, sir, that's only true if they needed to be hid from me sir, you understand," the peddler smiles. "Like last night, I'm sure the man's joke worked just fine, in spite of me seeing him."

"What did you see?" you ask eagerly.

"Oh, you was the victim, was you?" he laughs. "Well, this is how the man worked it on you. It was up in the room with the blue drapes." You realize he's pointing to the billiard room. "For 'alf an hour or so last night, there was a bloke standing between the curtains and the window. And you couldn't see him from inside so he surprised you, didn't he?"

"Was it about nine when he hid?" you ask.

"Aye, captain," he agrees, "I'd just heard the hour chimed when I first noticed the man.

You smile and mutter: "I'll surprise him," then slip the man another shilling. *Deduct 1 shilling from your Character Record.* You can barely conceal your delight. The murderer must have hidden behind the drapes when he heard Watson coming! **Check Clue Q.** **Turn to 124.**

372

You go on to explain that Marshall was also Symington's partner. Both Locke and Mycroft nod, interested in the information you have produced. "That makes your case stronger," Locke says. "Not only was Marshall a partner of Sir Terrence, he was also associated with another businessman of dubious principles. Marshall would not like his part in all this made public. It could ruin him." **Turn to 195.**

373

You are so eager to keep Marshall in sight that you crash into a boy selling papers. You apologize and tip him a sixpence to shut his mouth. *Deduct sixpence from your Character Record.* You hope the noise didn't catch Marshall's attention. He's ahead of you now, and seems to be walking faster.

- *If you continue following Marshall,* **turn to 463.**
- *If you quit and go to see Symington,* **turn to 265.**
- *If you quit and do not see Symington,* **turn to 520.**

374

Your ears prick up when Lewis mentions that someone recommended Sir Terrence's companies as sound investments. You wonder if Lewis recalls who suggested the investment to him. If someone were involved with Sir Terrence in his businesses, that man might have reason to kill Sir Terrence to avoid unpleasant publicity about their arrangements.

- *If you ask Lewis who recommended the investment to him,* **turn to 387.**
- *Otherwise,* **turn to 246.**

375

Watson bristles noticeably at the question. "She has no connection to this matter," he says sharply, "and I see no need to bandy a lady's name needlessly in such a case."

- *If you ask him who might have committed the murder,* **turn to 243.**
- *Otherwise,* **turn to 263.**

376

"There is another important piece of evidence about the Earl," you say, trying to cool the excitement in your voice. "The Earl gave the house to the club, and quite obviously, a man who owned the house for years is likely to know all its secrets. He could easily have used the trap door, found another place to hide, and then slipped away later. That possibility would match the evidence." **Turn to 471.**

377

"You were in the game of whist with Watson and Sir Terrence," you say slowly. "Could you describe the fight between them?"

Martin smiles and launches into a story he's obviously kept bottled up for hours. He begins with the last hand of whist and offers a card by card description of the play. "Watson was in rare form," he adds, "and outguessed poor Sir Terrence three times in the one hand of cards. When he was paying off afterwards, Sir Terrence commented that Watson must be able to read the cards through the back to play so well. Watson was livid when Sir Terrence made a remark about a lady friend of the doctor's."

"And that began the fight?" you interject.

"Oh, no, they had to blackguard each other another time or two before Watson punched him. I'd hardly call it a fight, really," Martin adds. "Watson threw the one punch and it was over." You think about what he has said. **Pick a number** *and add your Intuition bonus:*

- *If 2-7,* **turn to 415.**
- *If 8-12,* **turn to 530.**

378

For a moment you are excited to find the secret exit, but as you think about it, you conclude that the killer could hardly use this route. Even if he knew about the trapdoor, he would have needed a key to the secretary's office. Even if he met these requirements, he would have had to come out of the office without knowing whether anyone was in the hall. **Check Deduction 5. Turn to 282.**

379

"Now, Chambers," you say, trying not to upset the man. "Try to think very hard about the scene, and then tell me whether or not you saw the little table knocked over when you entered the room." **Pick a number** *and add your Communication bonus:*

• *If 2-8,* **turn to 155.**
• *If 9-12,* **turn to 514.**

380

Strickland looks down his list, and sighs deeply. "Thank goodness," he mutters, "we've almost finished this business. Next is Thomas Martin. He was in the whist game with Watson and Sir Terrence. Will you talk to him?"

• *If you interview Martin,* **turn to 537.**
• *Otherwise,* **turn to 239.**

381

"I am trying to get the course of last night's events clear in my mind," you tell Lawrence. "I would appreciate it if you would tell me what happened before you heard of the murder."

"Before the murder," he mutters. "Well, I'll do my best sir. I had had dinner at Simpson's, and then came around to the club just before nine. Almost immediately after I entered the lounge, I met a group of my fellow members talking excitedly about a fight over cards. Sir Terrence was among them, and I could see at a glance that he had lost the fight. He had a nasty lump in the middle of his forehead, and his clothes weren't sitting properly—obviously he'd been knocked down. Not long after I arrived, just a couple minutes before nine, he made his excuses to us and went upstairs. From the way he looked at the clock, it was almost as if he had an appointment with somebody. Who I don't know. I was looking towards the hall while I talked to the others, and saw Dr. Watson go upstairs a few minutes later, just after the clock chimed nine." **Turn to 101.**

382

"I will make this quick and simple," Locke says. "Christopher Marshall killed Sir Terrence. He was a silent partner in Sir Terrence's businesses. When it became evident that Sir Terrence was likely to be arrested for his latest project, Marshall killed him to keep him from talking."

"How did he do it, Captain?" McDonald asks.

"He slipped away from Watson, met Sir Terrence up in the billiard room, and struck him with the poker. When he heard Watson in the hall, he must have hidden behind the curtains. When Chambers found the body and fled, Marshall ran across the room and hid behind the door. From there he mingled with the others when they ran into the room. He made one mistake, however. He knocked down a little table crossing the room and dared not take time to set it right. Now, gentlemen," he says to you and McDonald, "you must find some constables and arrest him." Motivated by his commanding presence, you hurry to the West End of London and Marshall's home. **Turn to 338.**

383

"It is very important to remember whether that table was knocked over," you say slowly. "What I want to do, Chambers, is to review everything you did in the room, step by step."

"Yes sir," Chambers answers, his voice doubtful.

"Now set your mind to think things over," you say. "You saw Dr. Watson leave and went into the billiard room. Now take it from there."

"Yes sir," he answers. "I went in, and saw that the doctor had left a glass on the table by his chair, and a newspaper lying in the chair. I folded the paper neatly and put it on the table in front of the couch. Then I went over to do up the fire, and found that the poker weren't there."

"Very good," you say encouragingly, "very good. And where did you go then?"

"There was a bit of paper or something sitting on the billiard table, and I walked over to take care of that, and that's when I found Sir Terrence — That's it sir!" he says, with excitement rising in his voice.

"What's it?" Strickland asks.

"I walked right by that little table, sir, and I never would have left it lying on the floor. If it were knocked over, it must have been after I run out to yell for help. I guess one of the men who ran in later must have knocked it over."

"That must be the case," you agree. *Check Clue J.* **Turn to 439.**

384

"Could you tell me your opinion of Sir Terrence?" you ask the Earl. "I understand you knew him well."

"All too well," the Earl answers, "all too well. I must say that if some member of our club had to be murdered, the killer chose the right man."

"You were not fond of the man, sir?" you suggest.

"I hated him," the Earl answers cooly. "Aside from taking advantage of his friends and fellow members with his crooked business schemes, no decent woman was safe around the cur. He even made advances towards my wife." You wonder if the Earl knows others who hated Sir Terrence as much as he did.

• *If you ask him who might be the murderer,* **turn to 452.**
• *Otherwise,* **turn to 441.**

385

"Hear anything?" he answers thoughtfully. "No, I didn't hear anything," he says. "I'm certain we would have noticed any loud noises, because they would have disturbed our game. But the walls are very thick in this building, so you could have quite an argument without people hearing you across the hall. We only heard Chambers because he ran into the hall calling out." **Turn to 184.**

"There were a number of men who might have wished him ill," the Earl suggests. "Dr. Watson realized that Sir Terrence had defrauded him with his latest company. Alex Lewis despised the fellow. One of his business rivals, a man named Symington, was probably as delighted by the murder as I was"

"Any others?" you ask.

"Well, I would have an eye on Lord Howard, myself," he answers. "He acts like a fool, but he is far from being one. Sir Terrence did him out of a good deal of money, and his Lordship would resent that deeply. There might be others of course, especially if the cur tried to seduce someone else's wife, as was oft' said of him." *Check Deduction 18*. **Turn to 441.**

"How did you come to invest with Sir Terrence?" you ask Lewis. "Did it just come about because you were both members of the same club, or did someone suggest the investment to you?"

"Well, I knew Sir Terrence, of course," he answers, "but only casually. I didn't realize that he was in anything that might interest me until Christopher Marshall told me about it, and explained how well he was likely to do. Then I asked, and Sir Terrence let me in on his company. That was the New Zealand Tea Company. It was supposed to be a sure thing, but an unexpected storm wiped out every asset."

"But you invested with Sir Terrence again?" you urge. "In spite of losing money with him?"

"Well, I wasn't happy about it," he admits, "but Marshall told me the new company was much safer, and pointed out that Sir Terrence had just experienced some success in trading ventures to Barbados, while he scouted the terrain for his bigger effort. This was the St. Lucia vineyards, and they would have made us all rich if some volcanic ash from a neighboring island hadn't killed all the plants. After that I decided that the Ivory Coast Mining Venture could go on without me, and I didn't allow Marshall to change my mind." *Check Deduction 8*. **Turn to 246.**

388

The policemen take their positions, and you take yours, disappointed that you play such a small part in McDonald's plan. Suddenly, a door opens in the back of a shed in the back yard, and Marshall pops out and runs down the street. Yelling to the police for help, you start after him.

- *If you follow him, running as hard as you can,*
  turn to 100.
- *If you pause and try to outsmart him,* **turn to 146.**

389

You think of the trapdoor out of the room and wonder if the observant Sullivan noticed it.

- *If you ask him about the trapdoor,* **turn to 319.**
- *Otherwise,* **turn to 448.**

390

You wonder what details Howard can confirm for you.

- *If you checked Clue C,* **turn to 304.**
- *If you are finished questioning him,* **turn to 129.**
- *Otherwise,* **turn to 190.**

391

The police come to investigate, led by Inspector Gregson. He listens politely to your account of finding the body, thanks you for doing your duty by calling in the police, and rather pointedly bids you good day. As you obviously will not be able to do anything more here, you turn and leave. **Turn to 315.**

392

"Where was I?" Marshall asks, sneering. "Where do you think I was—upstairs killing Sir Terrence, while Watson was so busy with his paper that he didn't notice me? Why are you making such a mountain out of a piece of nonsense? I had private business at the time, business that has nothing to do with this case. But why waste time with such a lout as you?" He rises and turns to leave the room.

- *If you accuse him of murdering Sir Terrence,* **turn to 163.**
- *Otherwise,* **turn to 395.**

393

You decide to force open a basement window. Climbing the ivy seems too visible a way of entering the house. Someone might see you if you try that path. You find one basement window along the back wall of the house. It is partially hidden by bushes, and looks big enough for you to use. Silently, you try to open the window. **Pick a number** *and add your Artifice bonus:*

- *If 2-7,* **turn to 249.**
- *If 8-12,* **turn to 227.**

394

You sigh, and explain that you cannot figure out the code. "That's all right, lad," McDonald says with a smile. "I've figured it out myself. When Mr. Sherlock Holmes and I investigated the Birlstone murder, we ran across a similar code. If you number the words in Sir Terrence's flyer, and then substitute the numbered words into the note, you can read it." (*You may read the flyer at* **204**).

"But what does it say?" Mycroft asks impatiently.

"It a note for Sir Terrence to meet a man in the billiard room. Perhaps the other man was a silent partner in Sir Terrence's business." McDonald sighs. "Instead of paying him for silence, though, the partner used a more drastic method to keep Sir Terrence quiet." **Turn to 213.**

395

You watch Marshall hurry from the room and wonder if you could have questioned him more effectively. Strickland looks at you and shakes his head in disgust at your blundering. **Turn to 143.**

396

You hunt for the proper phrasing of your question. "If I understand things correctly," you say, "a group of gentlemen talked together in the lounge after the card game and the fight. Can you remember just who was in that group, Mr. Martin?"

Martin stops to think, then answers: "I cannot say with certainty, sir. We didn't stop to take notes, of course. I know Watson wasn't there, and Sir Terrence left after only a few minutes. Both the Howards were there, and I believe Alex Lewis was still around. Captain Lawrence came in right after I'd told the story of the fight once, and I had to repeat it for his sake. There may have been others." **Turn to 235.**

397

You remember that it was Johnson who told the police exactly when Dr. Watson went upstairs.

- *If you ask him how he knew,* **turn to 186.**
- *If you are done questioning him,* **turn to 181.**
- *Otherwise,* **turn to 260.**

398

"Now, Chambers," you ask, "I understand you saw Dr. Watson come out of the billiard room just before you went in. Can you tell me about that?"

"Yes sir, though I don't know what there is to tell," he replies, studying the pattern of the rug as he talks. "I was in the lavatory to see that there was plenty of clean towels, and when I came out I saw Dr. Watson come out of the billiard room. I figured he'd probably been in there by himself, and thought it'd be a good time to check the fire and fetch away his glass and such. No one else was in the hall or came out of the billiard room between the time he came out of the room and I went in."

- *If you ask him how Watson behaved,* **turn to 294.**
- *Otherwise,* **turn to 370.**

399

You reread the coded message, before you explain it.

- *If 162 186 119 correctly, 69 17 479.*
- *If you do not understand the message,* **turn to 557.**

400

"Now, if you walked in a room here," you say to Chambers, "and you saw a table like that lying on its side, wouldn't you have picked it up?"

"Maybe I would, sir," he answers, doubt very strong in his voice. "But if I could see there weren't nothing spilt, I might just take care of it in turn."

- *If you urge him to think harder about it,* **turn to 379.**
- *If you give up questioning him,* **turn to 439.**

401

Over the hum of voices you hear a sharp click, and then Marshall's voice ordering Symington, "Stand still!" You realize that the click was a gun being cocked!

- *If you rush into the room,* **turn to 200.**
- *Othewise,* **turn to 105.**

"Mr. Marshall, after Watson hit Sir Terrence, what did you do?" you ask.

"Oh, not much," he answers casually. "Mostly I stood around and chatted with some of the other members. We were still talking when Chambers began screaming about the murder, and all ran upstairs together." *Check Clue M.*

• *If you checked Clue O,* **turn to 503.**
• *Otherwise,* **turn to 308.**

"Who were you talking with when the alarm sounded?" you urge. "Which members were with you?"

"Oh, I don't know," Howard answers testily. "We'd been talking some little time and men drifted in and out of the conversation. We didn't keep a list you understand, though I know you detective chappies expected us to keep one."

• *If you checked Clue M,* **turn to 451.**
• *Otherwise,* **turn to 229.**

McDonald quickly puts a stop to any thoughts of celebration that you had. "That is all very interesting, sir," he says, "and I admit that I am pleased that I shan't be required to arrest Dr. Watson, but there is still a major problem at hand — whom am I to arrest? This is an important case, and I would appreciate your assistance in uncovering the true killer."

"Well, from the evidence and from what I have read of Sir Terrence, several names come to mind as killers," Mycroft suggests.

McDonald nods. "There is Mr. Alexander Lewis, who lost large amounts of money investing in two of Sir Terrence's schemes. The Earl of Waynesborough lost money with Sir Terrence, and he has been known to have argued with him. Finally, there is a man named John Symington, who conducts his business by the same methods Sir Terrence employed. Their competition had led to arguments, and there was bad blood between them. And a man like Sir Terrence may have had other enemies that we know nothing about."

"A good list, Mr. McDonald," Mycroft says, "but I think we can eliminate Symington as a suspect. It would have been almost impossible for a stanger to slip into that club. In addition, I saw a mention in the gossip columns of the Morning Chronicle that Mr. Symington was elsewhere last night. But what do we know of these men's motives and character? What do you have to say?" he asks you.

- *If you say more about Waynesborough,* **turn to 354.**
- *Otherwise,* **turn to 270.**

405

You realize that you will not learn anything more from Marshall. You thank him for his cooperation, and he replies graciously as he leaves the room. **Turn to 143.**

406

"You never recommended Sir Terrence's companies to anyone?" you repeat, the question plain in your voice.

"That's right," Marshall answers easily.

"Then why did some of your fellow members tell me very definitely that you had recommended Sir Terrence's firms?" you reply, a challenge clear in your voice.

Marshall doesn't flinch. "They must be mistaken," he answers. "They probably misinterpreted something I said, and then twisted the first mistake still more, until they were certain I recommended the investments. Very human of them." *Check Decision 9.* **Turn to 405.**

407

Before summoning the next witness, Strickland has Johnson bring in a light meal of apples, cheese, biscuits and sandwiches, insisting that you need a break from the stress of questioning witness after witness. Given his earlier hostility, you suspect that he is hungry himself. Once you have eaten, he consults his list and says that Captain Edward Lawrence, of the Royal Engineers, is the next witness.

- *If you talk to him,* **turn to 421.**
- *Otherwise,* **turn to 380.**

408

"Did Dr. Watson seem to behave differently or oddly when you saw him?" you ask. "Did he act like a man would behave if he'd just left a room with a dead man in it?"

"Oh, I don't know what to say, sir," he insists, "I really can't remember what he were like. I don't pay much mind to how the members are acting, you understand." **Turn to 370.**

409

You look at the coded note, and realize that you need a key to read it. You put it away carefully and look around the room.

The only place you haven't searched is Symington's desk. You'd like to look through it, but at the same time you should report the the violent death to the police as soon as possible.

- *If you call the police now,* **turn to 391.**
- *If you search the desk,* **turn to 225.**

410

"I have heard," you say to Symington, "that Sir Terrence had a silent partner in his efforts. I've also been told that someone helped him find prospects and funded his business. Do you know who this man was?" **Pick a number** *and add your Communication bonus: (Add 2 if you checked Decision 24.)*

- *If 2-7,* **turn to 110.**
- *If 8-12,* **turn to 193.**

411

"Did you see the fight between Sir Terrence and Watson?" you ask. "Can you tell me about it?"

"The fight?" he says, pausing to think, "Oh, the one over cards, earlier on. Well, I didn't see it myself, you understand, but one of the others told me later. I don't think you should make anything out of that sir, just a fight over cards. Sir Terrence was rather careless about using a lady's name, and Watson tried to teach him manners with his fist. This sort of thing happens all the time, you know: the old club would be very boring without such sport happening every now and again." **Turn to 130.**

412

"The killer was very careful," you say, "and he has not made it easy for us to identify him or even to learn that he was in the room."

"That's true," McDonald agrees, "I didn't see any evidence that anyone but Watson was in there last night."

- *If you checked both Clue J and Clue L,* **turn to 325.**
- *Otherwise,* **turn to 540.**

413

"Now Captain, I know you want to give us all the help you can," you insist. "Surely you can tell us something of the man. After all, you and he were members of this club. If we know what he was like we might understand why he was killed." **Pick a number** *and add your Communication bonus:*

- *If 2-7,* **turn to 255.**
- *If 8-12,* **turn to 549.**

414

"What does that `9 9:00' at the top mean?" McDonald asks. "It's set apart from the numbers, and doesn't seem to fit the code."

"I think I know," you say. "The `Three Continents' numbers its rooms, and the billiard room is number 9. So Sir Terrence went to room 9 at 9:00."

"That fits your other evidence very nicely," Mycroft agrees. "Some of your witnesses said that Sir Terrence acted as if he were watching the clock, and went upstairs just before nine."

McDonald nods, and looks gloomy. "The killer invited Sir Terrence up there to kill him, and set an appointment for death. The method used by the killer proves the premeditation. He had to pick up the poker from the fireplace and cross the room to kill Sir Terrence. If tempers had flared during an argument, the killer never would have been able to hit Sir Terrence from behind with the poker." **Turn to 213.**

415

You consider what other questions it would be wise to ask Martin. You wonder if he can remember which men talked together after the card game broke up.

- *If you ask who was in that group,* **turn to 396.**
- *If you are finished questioning Martin,* **turn to 570.**
- *Otherwise,* **turn to 235.**

416

"We found one very odd thing when we examined the room," you tell Marshall. "There is a trap door under the billiard table."

"A trap door," he laughs, "my, oh my, I wish I had known about that before. That's marvelous, sir, simply marvelous. All my life I've wanted a place with a kind of secret passage or hidden stair, and now you tell me that my own club has at least one. I say, Strickland," he adds, turning to the chairman, "once this investigation is complete, we had better turn the old club inside out to find what other surprises of that sort are here, eh?" **Turn to 310.**

417

The breeze tilts the man's hat up for a moment, and with a shock, you recognize Christopher Marshall, Watson's friend. You wonder why he is coming to see Symington. You know from the city directory that Symington has the only occupied office on the second floor. *Check Clue T.*

- *If you go away and return in an hour,* **turn to 265.**
- *If you hide and wait for the man to leave,* **turn to 165.**
- *If you follow the man upstairs,* **turn to 584.**

418

"You are certain, I gather, that the timing indicates that Watson was the killer?" you ask. "Why?"

"Well, timing is often a major problem for us, sir," the Inspector answers. "Clocks vary and men don't pay much attention to time because they don't know that a crime is taking place. But this time the witnesses were certain. Sir Terrence talked to several of the men downstairs after the fight with Watson, and then looked at the clock and hurried upstairs. The other men looked at the same time and remembered that it was a few minutes before nine, no more than three or four minutes. Now Dr. Watson took a glass of brandy from a waiter before he went upstairs, and the man remembers handing it to the doctor just at nine o'clock, because the clock was chiming. The doctor went straight upstairs, so there wasn't much time for someone to kill Sir Terrence and then leave the room. And there was no time at all between the time that Watson left the room and the other servant entered."

"I see," you say thoughtfully, and pause to consider your next question. *Check Clue A.* **Pick a number** *and add your Intuition bonus:*

- *If 2-6,* **turn to 456.**
- *If 7-12,* **turn to 524.**

419

The desk obviously is too plain and modern to hold any secret compartments. Finally, you pull out all the drawers and carefully examine the bottoms and sides. On the back of one drawer you find an envelope. The address reads: "To be sent to the police, in the event of my sudden death." It is signed by John Symington!

You try to decide what to do. It may be key evidence, but the police will be upset if you open it.

- *If you read it,* **turn to 567.**
- *If you send for the police,* **turn to 493.**

420

You look at the outline of the body without discovering anything of interest, then look over the billiard table with great care. Deep in one of the pockets you find a very odd scrap of paper. It has a string of numbers across it, with only one or two odd words. *(You may read the note at* **209** *and refer to it at any time.) Check Clue I.* **Turn to 558.**

421

Captain Lawrence comes in, a hard-faced, pugnacious looking man, striding with the firm, disciplined step of the professional soldier. When he seats himself at your invitation, he practically sits at attention. He obviously is not happy to be here, and you realize that you must choose your questions carefully.

- *If you ask his opinion of Sir Terrence,* **turn to 586.**
- *Otherwise,* **turn to 305.**

422

You decide that it's not worth the effort to search for a secret exit which may not exist. **Turn to 281.**

"No, sir, I never saw his face," you admit to McDonald. "I saw a man visit Symington's offices and decided to wait and follow him. He must have seen me and lain in ambush in the alley." You shudder with the pain in your head, and rub the sore spot gently.

McDonald sighs, obviously disappointed. "It's unfortunate you didn't see him," he says. "I thought the man who hit you might have some connection to Symington, so I went to see Mr. Symington myself. He was dead — shot in the back of the head. Well, you get yourself well — I shall pursue the case from here." You have failed in your investigation.

- *If you begin again,* **turn to the Prologue.**
- *If you want an explanation of the case,* **turn to 435.**

424

You get close enough to the man to see that it is Watson's friend Marshall. Just as you recognize him, he hails the only hansom in sight and is soon lost to view. You wonder what you should do next. *Check Clue T.*

- *If you go to see Symington,* **turn to 265.**
- *Otherwise,* **turn to 520.**

425

Watson thinks over the question, then shakes his head. "No, I can't think of who would have done it," he says. "One or two of the other members may have lost money investing in his company, but that's no reason for murder. Actually, my friend Marshall knew him better than I did. He might be able to come up with a name or two." **Turn to 263.**

426

"As you are certain that Watson did not kill Sir Terrence," you say to Sullivan, "who do you think killed him, or at least had reason to kill him?"

"Oh, Sir Terrence had a gift for making enemies," Sullivan replies. "He had cheated both Lord Howard and Alexander Lewis out of a good deal of money in his business shenanigans, and laughed at them on top of it. He also flirted with married women, and the husbands resented him for it, of course. The Earl of Waynesborough was especially vehement in his comments, I believe. And I'm certain Sir Terrence had business rivals who disliked him immensely." **Turn to 337.**

427

Watson looks startled at the question, then shakes his head. "I don't think it matters in the least," he finally says, and there is a certain sharpness in his tone. "I'm surprised that Sir Terrence had even heard of her, but we had the type of argument in which men try to hurt each other in every possible way. Bandying the lady's name about is just another example of Sir Terrence's rudeness."

- *If you ask who might have committed the murder,*
     turn to 442.

- *Otherwise,* **turn to 263.**

428

Taking all possible care, you search the office, hoping to find some clues to help in your investigation. **Pick a number** *and add your Observation bonus:*

- *If 2-6,* **turn to 544.**
- *If 7-12,* **turn to 322.**

429

You think about what more you might learn from Howard.

- *If you ask him what he saw when Chambers called out,*
     turn to 161.

- *If you are done questioning Howard,* **turn to 129.**

- *Otherwise,* **turn to 390.**

430

You study Captain Locke carefully while he is talking, and in spite of the care he has taken, you suuddenly see through his disguise. The Captain is Sherlock Holmes! You realize that it would be extremely untactful to admit that you have recognized him, and after a little more talk you prepare to leave. *Check Deduction 28.* **Turn to 244.**

431

You accept McDonald's invitation, and he summons a hansom and takes you to Symington's offices. You climb a flight of stairs and see a constable standing outside one of the doors. He salutes and steps aside when he recognizes McDonald.

Symington's office is an ordinary place. There are files against the wall on one side and a bookcase filled with oversize volumes on the wall opposite the desk. The desk is a plain, wooden one, with a comfortable chair behind it. A couple of wooden chairs complete the furnishings.

Symington's body lies crumpled behind the desk. He was a short, plump man, dressed in a very common brown suit. His skull is partially crushed by a bust of Wellington, which apparently fell from the bookshelf behind the desk. You kneel beside the body as McDonald examines the wound. "An odd death," the policeman comments. "The bust was always on the bookshelf right above the desk. The vibrations from some heavy wagon passing must have shaken it off, and it fell straight down upon the poor fellow." **Pick a number** *and add your Observation bonus:*

- *If 2-5,* **turn to 353.**
- *If 6-12,* **turn to 171.**

432

"I believe that Symington killed Sir Terrence," you say, "to eliminate a dangerous business rival."

Mycroft is the first to shake his head. "There is no way," Mycroft says, "that Symington could possibly be the murderer. He could not have made it into the club that night, and he hardly had sufficient cause to commit murder." **Turn to 525.**

433

"Reason for someone to kill him?" Strickland reiterates. "What sort of question is that? Obviously someone thought they had reason enough to kill him; otherwise we should hardly have to put up with all this nonsense. But I really don't see the point in gossiping about his strengths and weaknesses. He paid for them, poor man." **Turn to 228.**

Trying to apply all the thoroughness you learned from Sherlock Holmes, you search Symington's office. The files reveal nothing interesting. They contain letters and information customary to any business. Then you turn your attention to the chairs and bookcase. **Pick a number** *and add your Observation bonus:*

- *If 2-7,* **turn to 453.**
- *If 8-12,* **turn to 517.**

You are released from the hospital within a few days, though you feel very weak. To your surprise, Mycroft Holmes invites you to stay with him until you recover. He explains that he owes it to you since he involved you in the case.

That evening Dr. Watson visits so that he may tend to your injury. After he leaves you get the biggest surprise of the investigation. Mycroft comes into the room to see you, and with him is his brother, Sherlock. You gasp in amazement.

"No, my friend, I am not a ghost," Sherlock Holmes assures you. "It is not safe for me to be seen alive in London though, until a certain enemy makes a mistake that dictates his arrest. But when someone tried to blame a murder on Watson, I had to be certain that the matter was settled. When you failed, I assumed the disguise of Captain Locke of the Provost Marshall's office and investigated myself. Lie back, relax, and I shall tell you all about it.

"The murderer of both Sir Terrence Milton and John Symington was Christopher Marshall," Sherlock Holmes continues. "He was a silent partner of both of them. Sir Terrence threatened to ruin Marshall if Sir Terrence were prosecuted, and Marshall committed murder to protect himself. He silenced Symington for the same reason.

"He met with Milton in the club's billiard room at nine and killed the fellow with a poker. Hearing Watson's footsteps in the hall, he hid behind the drapes in the room and waited for an opportunity to escape. Marshall then hid between the door and the wall when Chambers went out in the hallway to call for help. As other men hurried into the room, Marshall slipped out from behind the door and mingled with them. It was a cooly executed job, by any standard.

He only made one mistake — when he ran from the drapes to the door, he knocked over a little table, and did not dare take the time to right it. Then, in the course of the investigation, he did everything he could to blur the facts. It was Marshall who spread the story that Watson was in love with Miss Phipps. Actually, the lady is a schoolmate of Watson's late wife. Watson took her to supper once, out of politeness, and then silenced a rowdy who heckled her while she preformed. It was a difficult case — only the most careful comparison of the witness' statements made it clear that he was not seen after the fight between Watson and Sir Terrence, and that Marshall had reason to commit the crimes." After the Holmes brothers leave, you recap the case and try to decide what you would have done differently. In your next investigation, you will not make the same mistakes. **THE END.**

436

You thank Captain Lawrence for his help, and he bows and marches out of the room. **Turn to 380.**

437

"Think back to last night, please, your lordship," you say, trying to set up your questions properly. "What were you doing when Chambers ran out of the billiard room calling murder? Tell me everything you can recall."

"Of course, sir, of course," Lord Howard answers eagerly, but then a puzzled look covers his face. "But you know, sir, it is very difficult to remember, because the sight of poor Sir Terrence was so shocking that it drove all previous events out of my mind. I shan't be able to give you a very detailed description."

"Don't worry, sir," you reply, "anything might help."

Lord Howard concentrates for a moment, then says, "I was downstairs at the time, in the lounge, talking to some of the other members. Just chatting about various things. We'd been going at it for some time when the servant called out, and we all ran upstairs. When we got to the billiard room, Sir Terrence was lying over in the corner, but I didn't notice much. There was too much noise and confusion and such. Then the police came, and we all went home very late."

- *If you ask who he was talking to downstairs,* **turn to 403.**
- *Otherwise,* **turn to 229.**

438

You chat a little longer with Symington, then thank him for his help. He bids you good day as you go out the door. **Turn to 315.**

439

You feel you've learned everything you possibly can from Chambers. He looks very happy when you tell him you're through and hardly waits for your thanks before leaving the room. **Turn to 515.**

440

You decide that it is not worth the effort to search the whole office. If there is anything interesting in the room it is probably hidden in Symington's desk.

- *If you search the desk,* **turn to 223.**
- *Otherwise,* **turn to 341.**

441

You realize that you will not learn anything more from the Earl and thank him for his time. He glances at his watch and says: "There is no reason to leave now. You would sit at the station for almost three hours, waiting for your train. You must stay for lunch."

You accept the invitation, and have a delightful meal, learning a few interesting facts about art, music and history from the Earl and his other guests. His driver takes you to the station in time for your train, and it is early evening before you finally arrive at Paddington.

- *If you checked Decision 9,* **turn to 486.**
- *Otherwise,* **turn to 366.**

442

"Do you know of anyone who might have wanted to kill Sir Terrence?" you ask, "anyone who had any motive?" **Pick a number** *and add your Communication bonus:*

- *If 2-7,* **turn to 425.**
- *If 8-12,* **turn to 461.**

443

With enough information to begin your investigation, you thank Mycroft and McDonald for their time. To lend some authority to your investigation, McDonald gives you a letter of introduction asking all who read it to cooperate with you. As you pull on your coat against the chill of the winter air, Mycroft stops you with a motion of his hand.

"There is one other matter you should consider carefully," he says. "Obviously you should see Watson first. But you might also want to see Mr. Christopher Marshall, a good friend of Watson's. He was the man who actually informed me of the doctor's difficulties. I then contacted Mr. McDonald. But Mr. Marshall may know a good deal about the case that he will tell someone working to save Watson. You might be wise to interview him before you visit the scene or talk to any other witnesses."

Wasting no time, you hurry to Dr. Watson's residence in Kensington. As soon as you send in your card, the maid leads you to the study to meet the doctor.

Dr. John Watson is a personification of the typical Englishman, a solidly-built man with a thick neck and strong jaw. Both his hair and mustache are carefully trimmed. His study is a comfortable room, with easy chairs, a snug fireplace and a glass-fronted bookcase. The case is well-filled, except for an odd-looking gap on the second shelf.

"Good day, sir," Dr. Watson says warmly. "I remember you well from the days when you assisted Mr. Holmes. And now you're a detective yourself. What can I do for you?"

"I hope to help you, doctor," you answer carefully. "Inspector McDonald of Scotland Yard and Mr. Mycroft Holmes have asked me to investigate the murder of Sir Terrence Milton."

"Sir Terrence?" he answers, surprised. "I thought last evening that McDonald was ready to hang me for that. Has he changed his mind?"

"He said," you answer carefully, "that all the evidence pointed to you, but he hoped I might find something he missed."

- *If you ask him to describe what happened,* **turn to 359.**
- *Otherwise,* **turn to 573.**

It occurs to you that there might be other information hidden in the note. "What do you make of it, gentlemen?" you ask McDonald and Mycroft. "What does the message mean?"

Mycroft thinks about it, then nods. "I think the note must have been written by a silent partner of Sir Terrence. Probably Sir Terrence was threatening to reveal his partner's share of the affair to the police, if the investigation ever came to trial. Obviously, the partner used the note to draw Sir Terrence to a place where he could meet with him quietly." **Pick a number** *and add your Intuition bonus:*

- *If 2-7,* turn to 213.
- *If 8-12,* turn to 414.

445

As you all stop talking, McDonald leafs through his notes and shakes his head. "None of these men has a solid motive for murder," he says. "At least, no reason known to us. Did you uncover any other suspicious behavior while you were at the 'Three Continents'?" he asks you.

- *If you checked Clue E or Deduction 8 and also checked Deduction 4, or you checked both Clues M and O,*
  turn to 487.
- *Otherwise,* turn to 157.

446

You remember that others said that Marshall had definitely recommended investment in Sir Terrence's companies. You wonder why he lied.

- *If you ask him,* turn to 406.
- *Otherwise,* turn to 405.

447

Strickland has written out a list of the witnesses and consults it now. "The next witness," he announces to you, "is Bobby Chambers, the man who found Sir Terrence's body. Will you talk to him?"

- *If you wish to talk to Chambers,* turn to 356.
- *Otherwise,* turn to 515.

448

You thank Sullivan for his patience and his helpful answers to your questions. He assures you that it was no trouble and that he is happy to have been of help. **Turn to 513.**

449

"What kind of man was Sir Terrence?" Strickland repeats. "Well, sir, he was not an angel, but then none of us is, now are we? As for the reasons for his death, I think almost any man alive has done something that someone else might consider grounds for violence."

"Do you have any idea what grounds Sir Terrence might have given?" you urge.

Strickland pauses, then decides to answer. "Yes, I can name one or two. He was not the most scrupulous businessman in London, and those who lost money with him may have resented the outcome of his schemes, though I think they should have accepted their losses as the price of their own gullibility. And at times he was a little careless in his attitude towards other men's wives, though as a gentleman, I can hardly name names, can I? Women and money: aren't those the most common grounds for murder?" **Turn to 228.**

450

When Chambers mentioned stirring up the fire, you began to wonder whether Watson would have needed to stir up the fire while he was in the room. Or did the doctor know that the poker had already been put to a less desirable use?

• *If you ask him if Watson would have needed to stir the fire,* **turn to 312.**

• *Otherwise,* **turn to 150.**

451

You remember that Marshall said he was one of the men in the group downstairs when Chambers shouted for help. You wonder whether Lord Howard could remember one man in particular even though he cannot name the group which was talking together.

• *If you ask him about Marshall,* **turn to 519.**

• *Otherwise,* **turn to 229.**

452

"Do you have any idea who might have killed Sir Terrence?" you ask the Earl. **Pick a number** and add your Communication bonus:

- If 2-8, **turn to 214.**
- If 9-12, **turn to 386.**

453

You find nothing of interest among Symington's books. You wonder if anything useful is hidden in Symington's desk.

- If you search the desk, **turn to 223.**
- Otherwise, **turn to 341.**

454

"The hidden partner may have been very anxious to stay hidden," McDonald says grimly, and turns back to the body. "Now how did I miss that?" he mutters. As you join him he points at a hole in the back of Symington's head, one that had been hidden by the pieces of the bust.

"Is that a bullet wound?" you ask. He nods. "Then Symington was murdered," you continue. "It almost certainly was the same man who killed Sir Terrence—the hidden partner," and McDonald nods again. **Check Deduction 21. Turn to 484.**

455

You catalog the evidence carefully, trying to remember if there is anything else that you should ask Sullivan.

- If you checked Clue G, **turn to 389.**
- Otherwise, **turn to 448.**

456

You carefully consider further questions. You wonder if it were possible for Watson to sit in his chair and not see the body.

- If you ask McDonald about this, **turn to 489.**
- Otherwise, **turn to 135.**

457

"Do you recall that the small table near the window was knocked over?" you inquire. "Was that already on its side when you entered the room?'

Strickland thinks a moment, then nods. "Yes, it was. I noticed it as soon as I looked away from the body. There was no one who could have knocked it over after I came in. I might have picked it up out of habit, if Watson hadn't urged us to leave the evidence alone." **Turn to 207.**

458

You realize that you have not learned much in the course of your visit to Baker Street. You wonder if there is anyone else you might learn about.

- *If you checked Deduction 19,* **turn to 238.**
- *Otherwise,* **turn to 170.**

459

You try to consider what further steps to take in the investigation. You are absolutely certain that there must be some evidence to prove Watson innocent, if you can only think of where to look for it. **Pick a number** *and add your Intuition bonus:*

- *If 2-8,* **turn to 422.**
- *If 9-12,* **turn to 364.**

460

The first blow misses, and you see Marshall ready himself to attack you again. "I'll teach you to meddle in my affairs!" he shouts. Before he can strike, you charge, hoping to wrestle him down before he can use that stick. *Check Clue T.* **Pick a number** *and add your Athletics bonus:*

- *If 2-7,* **turn to 526.**
- *If 8-12,* **turn to 551.**

Watson thinks a moment at his question, then smiles. "I have thought about that," he answers, "and I considered the evidence in the way that Holmes would have considered it, and the best conclusion I can come to is that I killed the man."

"What?" you gasp, then relax as he laughs.

"That is what the evidence indicates," he continues, "but as I know I didn't do it, I did think of two or three people who didn't particularly care for him."

"Who were they?" you ask eagerly.

"There's a man named Symington, with offices down near the river, who I heard spoken of as a very bitter business rival of Sir Terrence. Then there was the Earl of Waynesborough. There were rumours a few months back that his wife was overly friendly with Sir Terrence when the Earl was in Scotland on business. Of course, neither of them was at the club last night."

"Do you know anyone else?" you urge. "Anyone who might have lost money in his businesses for example."

"Oh, that's no reason for murder," Watson answers. "Cause for harsh words maybe, but not for a killing." *Check Deduction 3.* **Turn to 263.**

You stop as you read the flyer, nodding to the ragged man. "Is the show that good?" you ask, slipping the man a shilling. *Deduct one shilling from your Character Record.*

"Lord luv me, Guv, it's even better!" he exclaims. "Just ask your friends in the club there — many of them go around two and three times a week."

"Oh, so you work from this corner every night, do you?" you continue, and he nods eagerly.

- *If you ask him if he ever saw anything interesting at the " Three Continents,"* **turn to 529.**

- *Otherwise,* **turn to 124.**

You follow Marshall, hurrying a little to keep him in sight. He turns down an alley, and you rush even more. You don't want him to get away. When you reach the alley, he has vanished. It is a narrow, dirty strip of pavement, with the blank back wall of a building on one side and a high wooden fence on the other.

- *If you walk down the alley,* **turn to 535.**
- *If you go to see Symington,* **turn to 265.**
- *If you do neither,* **turn to 520.**

464

"Do you think the same man killed both Sir Terrence and Symington?" you ask McDonald.

The Inspector nods. "The hidden partner must have killed both of them," he says. "Sir Terrence threatened to expose him, and he then decided to kill Symington so that we could not talk to him. A brutal villain." **Turn to 484.**

465

You consider other people you should try to learn about from the commonplace books.

- *If you checked Decision 17,* **turn to 269.**
- *Otherwise,* **turn to 458.**

466

As you hurry down the alley, hoping you haven't lost your man, your eye detects movement at the top of the fence. As you turn towards it, you see a heavy walking stick swinging towards your head. Instinctively you duck. **Pick a number and add your Athletics bonus:**

- *If 2-7,* **turn to 526.**
- *If 8-12,* **turn to 460.**

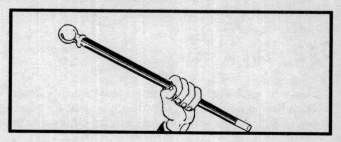

"It's rather odd that you say you were talking to the other members until the victim was discovered," you say pleasantly, and something in your tone makes Marshall straighten suddenly. "They do not recall your being with them, and several of them were certain when they named who was in the group."

"I hope you are not suggesting I lied to you," Marshall says, a hard note creeping into his voice. "A man who proposes to be a detective should always be suspicious of men who have exact memories of a matter of little importance. I remember them, anyway. The Howards and Captain Lawrence, and I believe that Martin and Lewis were there for a while. There may have been others; the murder rather drove such details out of mind." **Pick a number** *and add your Intuition bonus:*

- *If 2-8,* **turn to 308.**
- *If 9-12,* **turn to 362.**

468

You watch as the steam launch turns downstream upon the Thames and eventually disappears from sight. McDonald joins you, and upon hearing your story immediately gives orders to try to catch Marshall before he can leave the country. Then you and McDonald begin the return journey to Pall Mall to report that Marshall eluded your initial attempt to catch him. **Turn to 196.**

469

You put the papers back in their place and take one last look at Symington's desk. You feel there must be evidence somewhere. You study the desk, and try to decide where you might hide an extremely secret document. **Pick a number** *and add your Artifice bonus:*

- *If 2-7,* **turn to 138.**
- *If 8-12,* **turn to 580.**

470

You wait until after supper to go to Marshall's house. Hidden behind a tree across the street, you wait for him to leave. A little before seven he goes striding off towards the heart of the city, probably on his way to the club. You casually cross the street and examine the house. It is set in its own lot, surrounded by a brick wall about six feet high. Ivy climbs the walls of the house, and you can see that an upstairs window on one side is open a crack. There are also windows leading into the basement from the back.

- *If you climb to the open window,* **turn to 287.**
- *If you want to try a basement window,* **turn to 393.**

471

Mycroft silences the pair of you with a motion of his hand. "You say the man has a quick temper," he says, "but does that make him a proper candidate for a murder of this sort?"

"No, it might not," McDonald admits, "but it may be that the Earl only recently realized that Sir Terrence had cheated him. And even a hot-tempered man might take care in planning a murder."

- *If you checked Deduction 3 but not Deduction 5,*
  turn to 543.
- *Otherwise,* **turn to 270.**

472

"I of course didn't know Sir Terrence," you begin. "What kind of man was he? Do you think there could have been strong reason for someone to kill him?" **Pick a number** *and add your Communication bonus:*

- *If 2-7,* **turn to 433.**
- *If 8-12,* **turn to 449.**

473

"I found a very odd note on the billiard table," you tell Mycroft and show them the note. (*You may read it at* **209**.) They look at it, and glance at each other, a surprised look in their eyes. "Good work, lad," McDonald says. "I must have been asleep to have missed it when I searched. Have you broken the code?"

- *If you have broken the code,* **turn to 399.**
- *Otherwise,* **turn to 557.**

474

Though sniffing indignantly at the very idea, Strickland reluctantly hides behind the curtains of the middle window. You tell him that you cannot see him. "Oh, that is a very exciting discovery," he says sharply. "And I suppose that the killer who hid behind the curtains just walked out of the room while we were all looking at the body?" *Check Clue F.* **Turn to 583.**

475

You arise early the next morning prepared to continue the investigation. Today you will either discover who murdered Sir Terrence Milton, or admit failure in the case. You try to decide where to go first.

- *If you checked Decision 17,* **turn to 488.**
- *Otherwise,* **turn to 107.**

476

You stop suddenly in your examination of the books, shocked and confused by some of the items you noticed. The Daltons were killed in 1892 and the Bordens in '93. How could Sherlock Holmes have saved reports of events that occurred after his death? *Check Clue V.* **Turn to 148.**

477

You knock on the office door, and a quiet voice invites you in. A man who must be Symington is sitting behind his desk, and motions you to sit in another. The office is furnished very simply. It has only the most necessary furniture, books and file cabinets. The only decoration is a bust of Wellington sitting on top of the bookshelf.

"What can I do for you?" Symington asks. "Are you looking for a solid investment, sir?"

"I am looking into the murder of Sir Terrence Milton," you reply. "It has been suggested that you might help me clarify some aspects of the case."

"Sir Terrence's murder?" he asks surprised. "I doubt that I know anything, but of course I'll be glad to give you any help I can."

- *If you ask his opinion of Sir Terrence,* **turn to 261.**
- *Otherwise,* **turn to 550.**

478

As you examine the papers and files in Symington's desk, you notice that some of the files seem to be out of order. "Look at this, Inspector," you say. "These files are out of order. It looks like someone else must have searched them."

The Inspector shrugs. "If he had a hidden partner, the man must have wanted to keep his position a secret. We're probably too late to get the evidence."

You put the papers back in their place and take one last look at Symington's desk. You feel there has to be evidence somewhere. You study the desk and try to decide where you might hide an extremely secret document. **Pick a number** *and add your Artifice bonus:*

- *If 2-7,* **turn to 138.**
- *If 8-12,* **turn to 580.**

479

"This is how the code works," you tell the others. "It is based upon the flyer that Sir Terrence wrote for his last company, which is why he kept a copy of the flyer with him. If you number the words in the flyer, you can substitute the words for the numbers and read the note."

"What does it say?" Mycroft asks. You have a feeling he has already figured it out.

"It says, 'Milton meet me. A Thousand of Mines if you kept silent. Details when we meet. Has Cotton Ivory Speculative in most why Marshall safe.'" You hesitate as you finish reading. "The last part doesn't make sense," you mutter.

McDonald laughs. "If you write a note in code, it is normal procedure to fill up the paper, so that the arrangement of numbers or words does note give anything away. If your message is too short for the space you use, you just fill in with gibberish to confuse the man deciphering it." ***Check Deduction 15.*** **Turn to 444.**

480

"Well, Inspector," you say, "I think there is little doubt that this letter will serve its purpose. Marshall almost surely is the man who murdered Symington, and probably the man who murdered Sir Terrence. We had better arrest him at once." **Turn to 485.**

481

"You seem to believe that it is ridiculous to consider Watson a suspect in the murder," you tell Sullivan. "Why is that? All the evidence seems to point at him."

"You see," he answers, "you just put your finger right on it, right smack on top of it. Watson is not a fool, and he certainly would do a better job of murder than this, if he were to kill someone in cold blood. I don't say he would have been able to hide all the evidence, but he at least would have done it in a way that might confuse the matter. And aside from that, Watson would not kill a man in cold blood. It's totally out of character for the man. And if he lost his temper and smashed in the man's head in an argument, he would have summoned us himself, because it would be silly to pretend that he hadn't."

Pick a number *and add your Intuition bonus:*

- *If 2-6,* **turn to 337.**
- *If 7-12,* **turn to 240.**

482

"So Mr. Marshall was a partner of Symington," you comment. "I wonder whether he might also have been Sir Terrence's partner."

"We had better gather more evidence then we have before we try to make an arrest," McDonald replies. **Turn to 341.**

483

Marshall walks along at a good pace, neither hurrying nor dawdling. Then, he slows up, and summons the only hansom in sight. You see the cab rattle off towards the west end of the city, the area where Marshall lives.

- *If you see Symington,* **turn to 265**
- *Otherwise,* **turn to 520.**

484

So far you have been unable to find anything to identify any secret partners of Symington. You wonder if there is anything hidden in his desk.

- *If you search his desk,* **turn to 223.**
- *Otherwise,* **turn to 341.**

485

McDonald summons several constables to help him. You head for the western end of the city to Marshall's house, prepared to assist in the arrest of the murderer. **Turn to 338.**

486

A hansom takes you from the station to your rooms. You idly read an evening newspaper as your ride along.

- *If you checked Decision 14,* **turn to 495.**
- *Otherwise,* **turn to 366.**

487

You think about McDonald's question for a moment before answering. "I don't know if it's significant or not," you finally say, "but one witness lied to me."

"Oh, who was that?" McDonald asks, a trace of excitement in his voice.

"It was Watson's friend, Marshall," you answer, and explain the circumstances of the lie.

McDonald's excitement subsides somewhat, and Mycroft says, "That's hardly ground for a murder charge, is it? No two witnesses see the same event in the same way. There are always conflicts in observation or memory that may make one man appear to be a liar."

"Mr. Holmes is correct," McDonald agrees, "We know no reason why Marshall would want to kill Sir Terrence. Why, the man was in large part responsible for your entering the case. He wrote Mr. Holmes a note telling him what danger Watson was in. Would a murderer do that?"

"But why would he lie?" you ask again.

McDonald sighs deeply before answering. "He lied because he did not like being involved in a murder investigation, and he wished to make it clear that he could have had nothing to do with the matter. Probably most of the others lied a little too, but in ways you could not detect." **Check Decision 19. Turn to 157.**

488

You think about Sherlock Holmes' collection of indices and Commonplace books, still stored at 221-B Baker Street. You have Mycroft's permission to look through them. Is it worth the time and effort?

- *If you go to Baker Street,* **turn to 136.**
- *Otherwise,* **turn to 107.**

489

"Dr. Watson said he sat in a chair by the fire and read the paper," you say slowly, and McDonald nods. "Did you check to see if a man could sit in that chair and get up from it without seeing the body?"

"Yes sir, I did," the Inspector answers, "and I must admit that it is possible. The dead man was lying in the corner with a billiard table between him and the door. But there was a little table near the window knocked over, and I am certain that Watson would have set that upright—any man would. And from there he would have to be a contortionist not to have seen the dead man."

"Do you know when the table was knocked over?" you ask.

"No, I'm not certain." **Check Clue C. Turn to 135.**

490

You survey the alley. Something caught your eye along the fence a moment ago, though you see nothing now. You stand beside a gate in the alley way's high fence.

- *If you go through the gate,* **turn to 531.**
- *If you continue down the alley,* **turn to 233.**

491

After the initial shock of hitting the water's surface, you kick off your shoes and manage to swim back to the dock. There McDonald pulls you ashore. "I've already told my men to send orders to all the ports to arrest Marshall. Now we will have to make an embarrassing report to Mr. Holmes and Captain Locke." On the way to Mycroft's apartments, you order the cab stop at your own rooms so that you might change your clothes. **Turn to 196.**

492

"Mr. McDonald," you say quickly, as he finishes his instructions, "I should tell you that there is a secret exit out of the house. It exits out of the shed at the back of the lot," you add.

McDonald smiles. "Good work, young man," he says. "Then we shall change our plan. Moore and Lee will still knock on the front door, Andrews will take the back by himself, and the rest of us will wait outside the shed."

The plan works perfectly. A minute or two after the first knocks thunder against the front door, Marshall bolts out of the shed, straight into the arms of the burly Constable Reynolds. He is handcuffed without a struggle, and McDonald sends him off to Cannon Row, accompanied by the constables. "Mr. Holmes will be pleased," he says, smiling as he waves for a cab. **Turn to 231.**

493

You decide you had better not read the letter and instead send for the police. They come quickly, led by Inspector Gregson of Scotland Yard. You tell him what you found and hand him the letter. He thanks you for your help, bids you a good day, and almost chases you out of the office. Obviously he wants nothing to do with unofficial investigators. **Turn to 315.**

494

"Do you know anything about Alexander Lewis?" you ask your colleagues.

Mycroft shakes his head, but McDonald flips through a notebook and then nods. "I've known something of him for some time. We keep an eye out for his sort. He's a young man with too much money and too little brain, a bad combination. If the ones like that don't get themselves into trouble, they become prime marks for others. Lewis lost money investing in Sir Terrence's operations, but I am not certain that he has the intuition to know that he was cheated."

"Any hint of woman trouble between him and Sir Terrence?" Mycroft asks. "That's often a cause of violence, and Sir Terrence had a reputation for womanizing."

McDonald smiles. "It would more likely have been a grudge of Sir Terrence against Lewis than Lewis against Sir Terrence," he says. "Lewis chases women constantly. But unless he found out he'd been cheated and resented it, Lewis would hardly be likely to kill Sir Terrence. And he's so rich that he'd probably snub the man rather than attack him." **Turn to 201.**

495

You step down, pay the driver his 3 shillings, and enter the house where you maintain rooms. *Deduct 3 shillings from your Character Record.* Your landlord tells you that there is a gentleman waiting up in your room, and when you hurry up, you are very surprised to find Inspector McDonald sitting in your most comfortable chair.

"What brings you here, Inspector?" you ask. "Have you found some new evidence?"

"No, lad, not evidence," he replies. "But I received word that Mr. Symington has died in a freak accident which occured in his office just an hour ago. As his name came up in our talk yesterday evening, I thought you might like to go with me to see the body. There is something else too," he continues; "the nature of the accident was such that I have become suspicious. I sent word that the body should not be moved until we have a chance to examine it. There is a constable waiting for me there." You are shocked to hear of the death of a possible witness, but you doubt that it can have anything to do with your investigation.

- *If you go with McDonald,* **turn to 431.**
- *Otherwise,* **turn to 366.**

496

You wonder if Johnson saw anything odd when he went up to the billiard room.

- *If you ask what he saw,* **turn to 160.**
- *Otherwise,* **turn to 181.**

497

You notice nothing else of interest in your survey of the room. **Turn to 275.**

498

You think about what you have seen and cannot understand why Mycroft has spent the time and money to maintain 221-B as perfectly as he has done.

- *If you ask him why he did it,* **turn to 279.**
- *If not,* **turn to 244.**

499

Mycroft considers your failure, then says, "Captain Locke, I would appreciate it if you would look into this matter. I will send for you other gentlemen if he can prove who killed Sir Terrence."

Disconsolate at your failure, you return to your rooms. The next day at noon, a note comes asking you to return to Mycroft's rooms.

Once you arrive with McDonald, Mycroft explains that Captain Locke has solved the case. "Explain it to them, please, Captain."

- *If you checked Decision 28,* **turn to 382.**
- *Otherwise,* **turn to 109.**

500

You cannot think of an effective way to ask him the question.

- *If you urge him to think harder,* **turn to 379.**
- *If you decide he just doesn't know,* **turn to 439.**

501

You put the papers away and rise, feeling that you've learned everything relevant from Sir Terrence's records. "Thank you for your help," you tell Perkins.

His pleasant face hardens as he answers, "Just find the man who killed him. Just do that, sir, and we'll be more than even." You thank him again and leave. **Turn to 262.**

502

You finger the note from Mycroft, allowing you to look through Sherlock Holmes' books and records at Baker Street. If you are going to look at them, it is probably best to go at once, when Mrs. Hudson is sure to be home.

- *If you go to Baker Street,* **turn to 136.**
- *Otherwise,* **turn to 107.**

503

You recall that the witnesses who could name the members of the group who stood about and talked did not name Marshall. You wonder at the difference in the stories.

- *If you ask Marshall to explain the difference,* **turn to 467.**
- *Otherwise,* **turn to 308.**

504

"It does seem a rather drastic method," Captain Locke comments, "but if it comforts you and can afford the cost, I can see nothing wrong with your actions."

"Certainly nothing wrong," you agree, now addressing Mycroft. "I found it very useful today. It was amazing to see the amount of information that your brother compiled."

"Information by itself is of little help, though," Locke comments. "You have to reason through the evidence and use it in a logical manner." You chat a little longer, somehow reluctant to leave, while you try to make sense of what you saw at Baker Street. **Pick a number** *and add your Intuition bonus:*

- *If 2-9,* **turn to 244.**
- *If 10-12,* **turn to 168.**

505

With the letter, you know who murdered Symington. You quickly send for McDonald. He arrives with several constables in tow, looks at the letter and body, and leads you and the constables to the neighborhood in the West End of the city, where Marshall lives. **Turn to 338.**

506

You begin to walk towards the building where Symington has offices. His address is 118-D, and you can see a side door has that number over it. Perhaps stairs inside the doorway lead up. As you near the building you see another man slip into that door, moving carefully, as though he is afraid to be seen. He has his hat pulled down to partially shield his face from view. **Pick a number** *and add your Observation bonus:*

- *If 2-10,* **turn to 139.**
- *If 11-12,* **turn to 417.**

507

You think through what you know about the case and wonder what else Chambers might be able to tell you.

- *If you checked Clue C,* **turn to 545.**
- *Otherwise,* **turn to 439.**

508

You turn the evidence over in your mind, trying to think of anything useful Lord Howard might know.

- *If you checked Clue G,* **turn to 328.**
- *Otherwise,* **turn to 561.**

509

You hurry to the middle of the footbridge. You are in time, for you see a small launch coming down the waterway towards you; Marshall is visible on the deck. You try to decide the best way to stop him.

- *If you leap from the bridge onto the boat,* **turn to 185.**
- *If you call to the captain to stop,* **turn to 183.**

510

You wonder whether Howard knew about the trapdoor.

- *If you ask him about it,* **turn to 327.**
- *Otherwise,* **turn to 129.**

511

After reading the letter, you become very suspicious of the manner in which Symington met his death. You examine the body more carefully and discover that he was shot in the back of the head! The killer used the bust of Wellington to hide his work.

You immediately send for Inspector McDonald. He arrives promptly, accompanied by several constables. He looks over the letter, looks at the body, and immediately leads you and the constables to Marshall's house, hoping to catch the murderer before he flees the city. **Turn to 338.**

512

Since he is such an ordinary man, you are a little surprised that the indices list a reference to Christopher Marshall. You pull down the commonplace book indicated and flip through the pages. There is a clipping on Marshall, describing an incident in the western United States. When threatened, Marshall killed two men who accused him of cheating at cards. The story states that Marshall was freed on grounds of self-defense, though the Judge berated him for using unnecessary force to save himself. It mentions that he had left the town immediately. Another clipping mentions that Marshall has published a small monograph, "Secret Tunnels and Hidden Exits in the Modern House."

Below the clippings Holmes wrote, "Watson's friend and fellow club member. Trustworthy?" You wonder what this means, but you cannot be certain whether it matters or not. **Turn to 170.**

513

Strickland consults his list again, pauses to think, then nods. "The next man is Lord Howard," he announces. "He was downstairs talking with other members when all this was going on. Now, I hope you will treat him with the courtesy his rank deserves. Any of the signs of rudeness commonly associated with detectives will lead to the instant termination of the interview."

- *If you wish to talk to Lord Howard,* **turn to 271.**
- *Otherwise,* **turn to 137.**

514

"No one will hurt you, whether you remember or not, but please try to remember," you urge.

Chambers face screws up visibly with effort as he listens to you, almost as though he's trying to mentally retrace his steps. Then he smiles. "Yes," he says, "I can remember now, since you been so patient with me. The little table wasn't knocked over. If the furniture was tipped over like that, I would have gone straight to it and set it right, and made sure there weren't nothing spilt. And I would have seen Sir Terrence lying there from where that table sets, and I didn't see him until I went over by the billiard table looking for the poker."

"Thank you very much, Chambers," you say cheerfully. "That is valuable information." *Check Clue J.* **Turn to 439.**

515

The chairman looks over his list, stops to think, then nods. "I think the best man for you to talk to next would be Sir George Grant," he finally says. "He and Thomas Sullivan were playing chess in the room across the hall until Chambers began screaming, and they were the first members into the room after that. Sir George may have seen something we missed."

- *If you talk to Grant,* **turn to 286.**
- *Otherwise,* **turn to 278.**

516

"Who did you talk to after the fight?" you ask Lewis.

"Oh, how should I know?" he answers, a little frustrated. "It was just a group of us there, chatting together. I had to leave soon, anyway, as I was already late for an engagement."

- *If you ask his opinion of Sir Terrence,* **turn to 358.**
- *If you are finished questioning him,* **turn to 311.**
- *Otherwise,* **turn to 246.**

517

You examine the books very carefully, opening each of them and shaking them to see if anything is hidden among them. You find a very odd note folded and stashed in one of the books. When you unfold the sheet of paper, there is nothing on the note but numbers. It reads:

```
217  38   46   117  29   38   home
112  2    202  146  88   199  300
top  194  105  77   high 200  64
```

"What have you found?" McDonald asks, seeing your interest. You hand him the paper.

- *If you checked Clue I,* **turn to 253.**
- *Otherwise,* **turn to 156.**

518

You decide that it is impossible to learn anything from Symington and walk away from the building where he has his offices.

- *If you checked Decision 23*, **turn to 349.**
- *Otherwise*, **turn to 107.**

519

"Was Christopher Marshall one of the men you talked to?" you ask. "Watson's good friend."

"Oh, not just Watson's good friend, sir," he answers, "I think everyone who knows him thinks highly of the fellow. One of the best sort, you understand. Always helpful."

"Was he one of the gentlemen you were talking to when the alarm sounded?" you inquire.

"I'm not certain," he answers, "but I would imagine he was. I know I talked to him sometime last night, and I saw him in the billiard room right after the group of us ran in." **Turn to 229.**

520

You decide you've spent enough time on this aspect of the case. You won't bother seeing Symington.

- *If you checked Decision 23*, **turn to 349.**
- *Otherwise*, **turn to 107.**

521

You wonder if Sullivan had noticed the little table that was knocked over.

- *If you ask him about the little table*, **turn to 298.**
- *Otherwise*, **turn to 455.**

"Inspector McDonald," you begin, "I think it is safe to say that Sir Terrence's businesses were run in a less than honest fashion."

"Very safe," the Inspector agrees. "The man was a crook."

"Can you tell me of anyone who might have been his rival in the same sort of effort?" you ask. "If Sir Terrence were killed by an accomplice anxious to protect himself, a rival might be able to name him."

Mycroft and McDonald look pleased at the question. "A good idea young man," Mycroft says. "We discussed one such man when we talked of suspects, a man named Symington. Some flyers for his latest promotion came my way in the course of my work, and they seem very similar to those issued by Sir Terrence. While we dismissed him as a murder suspect, he'd be the best one to talk to, wouldn't he Inspector?"

"Yes, he would," McDonald agrees, and writes out Symington's address for you. ***Check Deduction 14. Turn to 187.***

523

Perkins pales. "What do you mean, saying I know about the master's business?" he asks. "I didn't know anything or do anything with his business sir, I just took care of him as it was my job to do."

"Don't worry," you say, quickly trying to calm him. "If you don't know anything about the papers, I will just go through them myself."

Perkins immediately agrees to this. He leads you into a study and shows you where the papers are kept. "I'll get you a pot of tea to make your work easier." **Turn to 575.**

524

You realize that a hidden entrance to the room might override the evidence of the timing. "Was the door the only entrance to the room?" you ask McDonald. "Did you search for any hidden exits?"

"There was only the one door," he answers, "and any man who went out the window would look very conspicuous. As for secret exits, it hardly seems likely to me in such a place. It's not worth the time to check into such a far-fetched idea, when the visible evidence is so solid." *Check Clue B.* **Turn to 456.**

525

You sink heavily into a chair, disconcerted by the knowledge that you have failed in the investigation.

- *If you wish to begin again,* **turn to the Prologue.**
- *If you want an explanation of the case,* **turn to 499.**

526

The heavy stick crashes down across the back of your head, and you fall unconscious. You awake in a hospital bed and are surprised to see Inspector McDonald sitting beside it.

"Well, lad," he says, "you finally woke up. Someone struck you a shrewd blow indeed. Do you know who did it?"

- *If you checked Clue T,* **turn to 106.**
- *Otherwise,* **turn to 423.**

527

"There was a little table knocked over in the room," you say. "It was the one by the armchair near the windows. Did you notice it?"

Marshall thinks a moment and smiles. "Yes, I saw it," he replies. "In fact, I began to pick it up until I heard someone talking about preserving the evidence. But it was knocked over when I came into the room."

- *If you checked Clue G,* **turn to 334.**
- *Otherwise,* **turn to 310.**

528

You think of the trapdoor under the billiard table, and you wonder whether Sir George knew anything about it.

- *If you ask him about the trapdoor,* **turn to 302.**
- *Otherwise,* **turn to 333.**

529

"Have you ever seen anything unusual at the club?" you ask, trying to keep your voice casual. "One hears stories, eh?"

"Well, that one is fairly calm on the outside," he answers, "but I think they have some odd goings-on inside. The police have to come now and again — they were here just last night in fact. And sometimes I see other signs that they have their fun. They must play all sorts of jokes on each other, I think."

- *If you ask him what he means,* **turn to 371.**
- *If you leave him,* **turn to 124.**

530

You wonder if Martin noticed exactly what Watson and Sir Terrence did after the fight.

- *If you ask him what they did,* **turn to 533.**
- *Otherwise,* **turn to 415.**

531

You pull open the gate and look along the inside of the fence. At the squeak of the gate hinges, a man hiding turns and looks at you in surprise. It is Marshall. With a cry of rage he turns and attacks you with his heavy walking stick. You charge also, trying to duck under the blow and grapple him, so that he cannot use the weapon. *Check Clue T.* **Pick a number** *and add your Athletics bonus:*

- *If 2-5,* **turn to 526.**
- *If 6-12,* **turn to 551.**

532

You realize suddenly that Captain Locke is actually Sherlock Holmes in disguise! No wonder he solved the case so quickly. **Turn to 382.**

"What did they do after the fight, Mr. Martin?" you ask, trying to sound casual. "Did they shake hands and apologize in the customary fashion, or was there another exchange of insults?"

Martin looks surprised at the question, then laughs. "Oh, they had no chance to do either," he finally says. "Sir Terrence stayed on the floor for a minute or two, trying to be certain that everything was still attached as it should be, and while Mr. Lewis and I made certain that he was all right, Chris Marshall hustled Watson out of the room. A smart idea on Chris' part too, to let them cool down a little bit. Just unlucky that when they ran into each other again, there was no one there to keep it from getting nasty."

"And what did Sir Terrence do after you got him back onto his feet?" you continue.

"We went into the lounge and had a go at the port," Martin replies. "There were some other fellows there and we chatted with them about the fight. Sir Terrence slipped off upstairs before long, and then I had to leave. I was to meet a friend for cards at the Bagatelle at ten, and I wanted to be on time. I played with Colonel Moran, and he insists that his companions be punctual. The old military values shining through, you know." ***Check Clue P.*** **Turn to 415.**

"Tell me what happened here last night," you urge, "beginning with the fight between Dr. Watson and Sir Terrence."

"First, I did not see the fight myself: I heard of it later, after we found the body. And it wouldn't have worried me if I had known, you understand. Those things will happen when you have a number of energetic and proud men in a club. As long as they don't damage the furnishings, we expect a little brawl now and then. It's in the nature of our membership—to join a man must have visited at least three continents, and such men tend to be lively fellows." **Pick a number** *and add your Intuition bonus:*

- *If 2-7,* **turn to 301.**
- *If 8-12,* **turn to 562.**

535

You turn and hurry down the alley, hoping to see Marshall when you reach the end of it. **Pick a number** and add your Observation bonus:

- *If 2-5,* **turn to 233.**
- *If 6-7,* **turn to 466.**
- *If 8-12,* **turn to 490.**

536

You consider the various tasks that lie ahead of you today, wondering what you should do first and which actions are not worth doing at all. It seems to you that your first action should either be to look at Sherlock Holmes' records in his old Baker Street rooms, or to visit Sir Terrence's business rival, John Symington.

- *If you go to Baker Street now,* **turn to 264.**
- *If you go to see Symington,* **turn to 357.**
- *If you decide to see neither of them,* **turn to 107.**

537

Martin comes into the room, a slender, brisk man with white hair and bright eyes. He's obviously eager to talk. "So they've engaged you to look into last night's murder, have they?" he laughs. "Well, I would have thought that this was one case the Scotland Yard men could solve without help."

"It appears simple to you, then?" you reply, hoping to draw him out.

"Well, I hate to say it, because he's a nice man," Martin says, "but it looked painfully obvious to me that John Watson murdered Sir Terrence. Just bad luck, I would say. Sir Terrence outraged him when we were playing cards. Watson left to cool off. I think they found themselves in the billiard room by accident and probably took up their argument again. With no one else around to control them, it ended in tragedy."

- *If you ask him to describe the fight,* **turn to 377.**
- *If you don't ask him any more questions,* **turn to 570.**
- *Otherwise,* **turn to 415.**

538

You wonder why he finds it so absurd that Watson should be suspected of the murder.

- *If you ask him to explain his comment,* **turn to 481.**
- *Otherwise,* **turn to 337.**

539

You wonder if any of Sir Terrence's rivals might have any insights into the murder, or perhaps have had something to do with the killing.

- *If you ask about others in the same business,* **turn to 522.**
- *Otherwise,* **turn to 187.**

540

McDonald listens to the evidence and says sharply, "Come man, you must have found something more decisive than you've shown so far. As it is, I cannot justify delaying Watson's arrest."

"Patience, Inspector," Mycroft says. "Let the young man describe all the evidence." Though beginning to feel desperate, you go on telling what you saw and heard.

- *If you checked Clues F, J or Q,* **turn to 153.**
- *Otherwise,* **turn to 268.**

541

In your perusal of the basement, a shelf in the corner strikes you as odd. You wonder if it hides anything; you are certain that Marshall wouldn't keep any important papers in the basement.

- *If you explore the shelf more closely,* **turn to 164.**
- *Otherwise,* **turn to 323.**

A clock chimes softly from Mycroft's bedroom, and you realize it is getting late. "What course of action will you follow tomorrow?" Mycroft asks.

"I haven't decided yet," you admit. "There are several sources of information I might explore. I would like to know more about the lady who was mentioned so prominently in the argument between Sir Terrence and Dr. Watson. Has your friend Captain Locke discovered anything about her?"

"He has not reported to me yet," Mycroft replies. "I shall send you a note as soon as he does."

"Do you have any suggestions? Who should I see first?" you ask. "Perhaps I should visit Sir Terrence's home to look for evidence there?"

"That can wait," McDonald says. "Sir Terrence won't return to destroy any evidence." He pulls a *Bradshaw* down from Mycroft's shelves and consults the railroad schedules. "I was right," he says. "If you wish to see the Earl of Waynesborough, you had better go out to his estate first thing tomorrow. The only trains that will make the connection leave Paddington at eight in the morning and four in the afternoon. If you go, you will spend most of the day getting there and returning."

You thank Mycroft and McDonald for their help and return to your own lodgings. Sleep is slow in coming as you figure out what to do first the next day.

- *If you decide to go and see the Earl,* **turn to 554.**
- *Otherwise,* **turn to 242.**

"I learned something else important about the Earl," you say quietly. "Some of the other men at the club told me that Sir Terrence had dallied with the Earl's wife. That might be enough to make many a man turn to murder, more so for a man with a hot temper."

"Aye, that it would," McDonald replies. "I had heard that he was out at his country house last night, but perhaps he slipped away from his guests. I understand that Lord Grayson rather than the Earl was the host of the affair." **Turn to 270.**

544

You search all of the room except for Symington's desk, but do not find anything that will help your investigation. Frustrated, you search the desk. Should you search further before you call in the police?

- *If you send for the police now,* **turn to 391.**
- *If you search the desk,* **turn to 225.**

545

You remember the little table that was knocked over in the billiard room. You realize that if Chambers can say definitely that it wasn't knocked over when he went in, it would be a very strong piece of evidence that Watson could have been in the room without seeing anything suspicious.

- *If you ask Chambers about the table,* **turn to 320.**
- *Otherwise,* **turn to 439.**

546

Hurrying away from Symington's office, you send word of what has happened to McDonald. The Scotland Yard man joins you soon, accompanied by several constables. Together you leave for Marshall's home in London's West End. **Turn to 338.**

547

"Did you see the fight between Dr. Watson and Sir Terrence?" you ask.

"I didn't exactly see it, though I was in the room," Lewis replies.

"What do you mean?" you ask.

"I was sitting in the corner, reading a paper, while the others were playing whist. I tried to ignore it when Watson and Sir Terrence began insulting each other, but I found I couldn't. As I looked up to try and quiet them, I saw Sir Terrence falling over backwards. Watson went off somewhere, and the rest of us chatted together in the lounge for a while."

- *If you ask him who he talked with,* **turn to 516.**
- *Otherwise,* **turn to 347.**

"I am pleased you could talk to me," you say to Marshall. "I would appreciate it if you could describe the argument between Dr. Watson and Sir Terrence."

"Ah, you are starting at the beginning," he chuckles. "Very well. We had been playing for some time, and I must say that Watson played much better than he usually does. He outplayed Sir Terrence several times. Finally, Watson and I won the rubber with a slam on the last hand, and he made two finesses through Sir Terrence's hand that were almost miraculous."

"And Sir Terrence commented about it?" you ask.

"He did indeed," Marshall answers. "He said that Watson could read the back of the cards as well as the front, then Watson answered that Sir Terrence had just been outplayed.

"At this point, things got nastier. Sir Terrence passed a comment about Watson's current ladyfriend, and I thought we would have a fight right there, because Watson is very protective of his lady's honour. But instead, Watson made a comment about Sir Terrence's misrun companies costing him money, and Sir Terrence called him a fool. Then Watson knocked him down with one blow. Fortunately, Watson left the room before Sir Terrence got up for another round."

- *If you checked Clue P,* **turn to 222.**
- *Otherwise,* **turn to 112.**

"Persistent, aren't you," he growls, then smiles. "I suppose that is a necessary quality in your profession. The reason I don't know very much about my fellow member, Sir Terrence, is that I have spent the last two years building bridges with the army in Africa. Even before that I didn't associate often with Sir Terrence. My older brother lost heavily investing in speculative businesses, and I decided to have as little as possible to do with men in that business, for fear they would lead me into the temptations that ruined my brother."

"I see," you answer quietly. "Thank you for explaining matters so clearly." **Turn to 305.**

550

You consider what questions to ask Symington. Could he know who helped Sir Terrence in his promotions?

- *If you ask who helped Sir Terrence,* **turn to 410.**
- *Otherwise,* **turn to 564.**

551

You grapple with Marshall, trying to trip him up. At the same time you call for the police. Desperate to be free of you, he hooks your ankle with the end of his stick, trips you, and takes to his heels as you fall to the ground. You chase him, but he seems to know this section of London well and finds his way to a main street while you're still half a block behind him. There he takes the only hansom in sight and escapes.

Where your legs have failed, you apply your mind to the problem. You tell a bobbie what has happened, and he quickly sends for McDonald. The Inspector arrives soon. He listens to your story, then nods grimly. "I think we had better nab Mr. Marshall," he says. "We'll go to his house now." With several constables to help, you hurry towards the west end of the city and Marshall's home. **Turn to 338.**

552

"I cannot say that I really knew the man," Symington says, suddenly nervous. "We hardly associated with each other and never worked together."

"Surely you must know something," you urge.

"No, I cannot say that I do," Symington insists. "We just didn't have anything to do with each other. We didn't run our businesses in the same fashion, you understand." Before you can ask more, Symington looks at his watch and says: "Oh dear, I didn't know how late it was. You must excuse me, I have an important appointment across town." He almost pushes you out the door in his flurry. Reluctantly, you leave the building. **Turn to 315.**

553

"I think Chambers, the servant, killed Sir Terrence, and then screamed for help when he 'found' the body," you say. "Probably Sir Terrence hid when Watson entered the room, not wanting another confrontation. Then, after Watson left the room, Chambers went in and brained him. Sir Terrence, unkind man that he was, must have given him some grounds for the crime."

All three men shake their heads. "No, no," Locke says, "that is just not possible. There is no evidence that Chambers has a motive. And in addition to that, the evidence indicates that Sir Terrence had been dead for some time when the body was found." **Turn to 525.**

554

Though you slept poorly due your excitement, you rise early the next morning. After a brief breakfast in your rooms, you hurry to Paddington to catch your train. It is on time, and you are able to make your connection south to the village of Waynesborough (which gave the Earl his title). A dogcart takes you to the Earl's manor. The butler looks at your letters of introduction and after only a few minutes wait you are taken in to meet the Earl. The Earl is a tall slender man, very distinguished looking, wearing a monocle in one eye.

"Good day, sir," the Earl says. "How may I help you?"

"As you can see from my letter of introduction," you say, "I am investigating the murder of Sir Terrence Milton, who was killed in 'The Three Continents Club' the night before last. I understand that most of the members were your guests that evening?" you ask.

"Yes, mine or my son's. I checked the list with the butler, because we were hard put to find rooms for all of them. All of them came, and none of them could have gone to London again that evening. The trains are impossible."

"And you were with them all the evening yourself?" you ask.

"Not all the time," he answers, "But I was here at nine

o'clock. We were exchanging toasts after dinner at that time, and the papers tell me that the body was discovered at nine-thirty." You make a note or two, and consider further questions for the Earl. *Check Decision 20.*

- *If you ask his opinion of Sir Terrence,* **turn to 384.**
- *If you have no more questions for him,* **turn to 441.**

555

"Confound the rascal!" Watson cries, following you down the narrow stairway. **Turn to 596.**

556

"What did I think of Sir Terrence?" Watson repeats. "Well, I didn't really think much of him, one way or the other. One doesn't have much opinion of every man he meets, after all, and he was just a casual acquaintance."

"But his business failure cost you a lot of money, didn't it?"

"Hardly reason to hate a man," Watson answers. "I knew it was a risky venture. I may have thrown it up at him last night, when we were employing every insult that occurred to us. You know sometimes men who don't really know each other get in a shouting match, and you throw everything you possibly can at the other fellow."

"So you didn't care for him or dislike him?" you continue.

"No, not at all. I wish he had been murdered in a way that did not involve me. Aside from that, I have no opinion of his character whatsoever. I am not at all certain that he had a chaacter, to be frank." **Turn to 361.**

557

You study the code, wondering at this strange mix of numbers and words. Perhaps, you need some other document to decipher the message. You try to remember everything you know about secret codes. **Pick a number** *and add your Scholarship bonus:*

- *If 2-8,* **turn to 394.**
- *If 9-12,* **turn to 182.**

You tell Strickland that you are finished examining the billiard room and now wish to interview the members and staff who were present about the time of the murder. Nodding in agreement, he leads you to a small office on the first floor. A desk and several comfortable chairs make it an ideal place for interviews.

"How many people were in the club last night?" you ask, wondering how long the interviews will take.

"We are fortunate in that regard," he answers stiffly. "Lord Grayson invited all the members to his estate for a few days' entertainment, and most of the membership accepted. The members here last night were myself, Dr. Watson of course, Sir Terrence, Mr. Christopher Marshall, Lord Howard, Mr. John Howard, and Edward Lawrence. Sir George Grant and Mr. Thomas Sullivan were playing chess in the study across the hall from the billiard room, while Mr. Thomas Martin and Alexander Lewis were here earlier, but both left before the body was found. Two of the servants might help you some. Johnson saw Dr. Watson go up to the room and Chambers was the man who found the body. I will stay here to witness what is said, if you wish."

- *If you wish to question Strickland,* **turn to 285.**
- *Otherwise,* **turn to 352.**

You take a hansom to Sir Terrence's townhouse, hoping to find some evidence to clarify the case. A servant answers the door. "May I help you, sir?"

"Yes," you answer. "I am investigating the tragic murder of your late master, Sir Terrence. There are those who fear that Scotland Yard will not devote their entire efforts to the case." You hand the man your credentials, which he reads very carefully.

"What may I do to help?" he asks. "My name is Perkins. I was Sir Terrence's personal servant, and he treated me very well. I'd give all I had to see the devil who murdered him swing for it."

- *If you ask to look through Sir Terrence's papers,*
    turn to 226.
- *If you ask Perkins to help you look through the papers,*
    turn to 343.
- *If you have a pound you may offer him money
    to see the papers,* **turn to 574.**

560

Late that evening, you go to Mycroft's room to explain the case. (You had received a note from him, asking that you wait until eleven to visit. A matter of importance had come up, and Mycroft's services were required.)

When he lets you in, you find that McDonald and Captain Locke are there before you, both anxious to hear if you've found the murderer. At the urging of all three men, you carefully explain the evidence, then announce your conclusion.

- *If you admit that you don't know who killed Sir Terrence,*
    turn to 121.
- *If you accuse Watson,* **turn to 303.**
- *If you accuse the Earl of Waynesborough,* **turn to 221.**
- *If you accuse Marshall,* **turn to 115.**
- *If you accuse Symington,* **turn to 432.**
- *If you accuse Chambers, the servant who found the body,*
    turn to 553.

561

Satsified that you have learned everything possible from Lord Howard, you thank him, and he leaves the room. **Turn to 137.**

562

You wonder who considered the fight important enough to mention it to Strickland after the shocking discovery of Sir Terrence's body.

- *If you ask him who told him,* **turn to 257.**
- *Otherwise,* **turn to 301.**

"I never met Sir Terrence Milton," you say slowly, "and I cannot say that I know much about him. Can you tell me anything about what sort of man he was?"

McDonald starts to shake his head, then stops. "Aye, I can talk now," he says slowly. "When he was alive I had to be careful, to avoid an action for slander. Sir Terrence promoted businesses, and at best he didn't worry very much about whether the business was genuine or not. He had a pattern. He would promote and sell out a small business that did very well, then attempt something big that failed. The last attempt at a big business, the Ivory Coast Mining Venture, was so patently fraudulent that we were investigating it closely in spite of Sir Terrence's rank and family. Those who invested in it lost everything, a total of some six thousand pounds."

"In short, Sir Terrence was a crook," Mycroft adds.

"A crook and a mean-spirited man," McDonald continues. "He was the sort of man who was not only dishonest himself, but also believed every other man was dishonest." He searches in his pocket. "Here, take this," he says, handing you a colorful flyer. "This is the promotional sheet he had printed up for the Ivory Coast Company."

This flyer is copied in paragraph 204. You may read it there any time you wish. ***Check Clue D.*** **Turn to 443.**

564

"Had you heard of Sir Terrence having any problems with business associates?" you ask. "Anything that could have led to his murder?"

"Oh, I really couldn't say," Symington answers. "There are so many stories about every entrepreneur that you would think all of us were going to be murdered before the year is out." He laughs and turns the conversation back to investments. You can see that you will learn little from him. **Turn to 438.**

565

Opening the door, you enter the office and discover a gruesome sight. The body of a man who must be Symington lies behind the desk, a heavy, bloodied bust of Wellington across the back of his head. It appears to have fallen off the bookshelf and killed the unlucky man. How utterly bizarre!

- *If you checked Clue T,* **turn to 108.**
- *Otherwise,* **turn to 177.**

566

"What did I think of Sir Terrence?" Watson repeats slowly. "Well, I could hardly say, could I? One mustn't speak ill of the dead. I had bad luck when I invested in his company, but then, I suppose he had worse luck himself. No, I can't say much more—I just didn't consider him one way or the other." **Turn to 361.**

567

You carefully open the envelope and read. The text is startling:

Metropolitan Police, Scotland Yard

Sirs,

As you may know, I have operated my businesses in an illegal and fraudulant manner, designed to take advantage of the most credulous segment of the public.

I neither boast of, nor apologize for, these activities. By the time anyone reads this letter, I will be beyond the reach of human judgment. My purpose in writing is to insure that my partner in these endeavors does not escape the law. If I die suddenly and violently, he will almost surely have murdered me. He has given me the money to finance my initial operations, has referred investors to me, and has taken a large percentage of the profits. His name is Christopher Marshall, of London.

John Symington

You wonder what to do with this amazing document. *Check Clue S.*

- *If you checked Deduction 21,* **turn to 505.**
- *Otherwise,* **turn to 511.**

568

Alexander Lewis comes into the room and takes a chair without being asked. He is a tall handsome man, with dark, thick hair. He seems younger than most of the men you've interviewed. You have the feeling that he is not one of the intellectual leaders of the club.

"Well," he begins, "I wasn't sure if you'd see me or not, sir, and I'm very pleased you decided to see me."

"Oh?" you reply, a touch surprised. "Why is that?"

"Well," he answers, smiling, "You know I wasn't here when they found Sir Terrence's body, so I didn't see anything that could really be called evidence. But I'm excited anyway, don't you know, for I've never talked to a detective before." You pause to consider the best questions for this cheerful soul.

- *If you ask if he saw the fight,* **turn to 547.**
- *If you don't wish to question him further,* **turn to 311.**
- *Otherwise,* **turn to 347.**

569

You think through what Lawrence has said to you and wonder whether you should ask him about anything else.

- *If you have finished talking to Lawrence,* **turn to 436.**
- *If you checked Clue C,* **turn to 582.**
- *Otherwise,* **turn to 116.**

570

You can think of no further questions for Mr. Martin and you thank him for his time and cooperation. It has been a pleasant talk, regardless of whether or not you learned anything of value in the course of it. **Turn to 239.**

571

You study the room again, and convince yourself that there is no possible hiding place you have missed. Either Marshall is innocent or he is too careful to keep any incriminating records in his home. You sort through all the records you have examined, looking for what you might have missed. Then you realize that while you saw a box of old checks, you didn't look at them individually.

Quickly you pull the box out and leaf through the checks one by one. Only one is of any interest. On January 1, 1893, Marshall had written a check for 300 pounds, payable to Sir Terrence. **Check Clue Z.**

- *If you checked Clue W,* **turn 252.**
- *Otherwise,* **turn to 348.**

572

"Captain, that man is a murderer!" you shout, pointing at Marshall. "Seize him!"

"So that's why all the coppers are coming this way," the burly captain exclaims. "Jonesey, Pete, hold onto the rascal!" he orders. As Marshall turns, hoping to dive into the water and escape, one man knocks his legs out from under him with a spectacular dive. Two other crewmen grab Marshall's arms and bind him with rope before he can get to his feet. The captain then steers the launch back to the dock as a panting Inspector McDonald arrives. The constables take Marshall to Cannon Row, while McDonald congratulates you and thanks the captain. Then you and McDonald head for Pall Mall to report to Mycroft Holmes and Captain Locke. **Turn to 231.**

573

"Did you know Sir Terrence well?" you ask Watson.

"No," he answers, "I can't say I knew him well. I saw him in the club occasionally, but he was neither a particular friend of mine, nor an enemy."

"But you invested heavily in his company?" you continue.

"Well, one doesn't know every business associate," he answers, a little testy. "I heard that he was involved in a promising venture and took a chance on it. That's all." **Pick a number** *and add your Intuition bonus:*

- *If 2-6,* **turn to 332.**
- *If 7-12,* **turn to 216.**

574

You offer a pound note to Perkins as you ask to look in Sir Terrence's papers. To your surprise, the man recoils in horror. "Money to look through the master's papers?" he asks. "Not on your life sir, I can't be bought. You're up to no good, I'll be bound, and I'll not let you set a foot in his house!" Before you can even begin to recover, he closes the door firmly in your face. **Turn to 262.**

575

You begin to go through the piles of papers. They are neatly organized and docketed. There is nothing to indicate who helped him in his ventures. The only evidence that mentions anyone whom you met is a note from Marshall, acknowledging that Sir Terrence had repaid a loan of 3000 pounds on the last day of 1893. *Check Clue W.* **Turn to 501.**

576

Marshall's colour deepens; he tries to say something, then stops. "But, how did you find out? My God!" Breaking his momentary trance, he turns and runs out the door. You follow, but he is out of the club and swinging onto a passing hansom before you can lay a hand on him. Not another cab in sight!

"What shall we do now?" Strickland demands. "The man confessed, but he's getting away."

"He won't get far!" you reply, quickly dashing out of the room. You hastily make your way to Mycroft Holmes' apartment, and to your delight find that Inspector McDonald has arrived for the evening's meeting on the case. As you explain Marshall's admission and flight, he swings into action. With several bobbies to help with the arrest, he hurries towards Marshall's home. Will you arrive in time? **Turn to 338.**

577

"Murderer!" the captain laughs, "Tell me another one, mister. I know Mr. Marshall is an honest man, and he paid me well. Pick up speed, Jonesy," he orders. **Turn to 468.**

As you think the problem over, you decide that there are two ways that you might stimulate Chambers' memory. You could force him to retrace his steps in the room, action by action, or you could ask him whether he would have left the table lying on its side if he had seen it in that situation.

● *If you ask him to retrace his steps,* **turn to 383.**

● *If you ask if he would leave it lying there,* **turn to 400.**

579

"You mentioned a man named Symington," you say to McDonald. "What do you know about him? Did he have any motive to kill Sir Terrence?"

McDonald smiles and says, "If he had motive, then half the businessmen in London may commit murder tomorrow. Symington is the same sort of man that Sir Terrence was, without the glitter of inherited rank and influence, though Symington is a little bit sharper. I tend to think that most of the companies he promotes actually exist, whereas, we suspect that Sir Terrence's efforts consist of a promotional flyer and a bank account. The two had argued with each other from time to time, like two vultures who wanted to eat the same carrion."

"I thought we had decided that Symington had been cleared," Mycroft interjects. "Why waste time over him?"

You think a moment, then answer, "He might be useful to talk to, anyway. A rival often knows the ways of a man better than his friends." ***Check Deduction 14.*** **Turn to 445.**

You try to think where you would hide something in this sort of desk. It is a very ordinary piece of furniture, and obviously doesn't have any secret compartments. Then you nod to yourself in satisfaction. One by one you pull all the drawers all the way out, and look at their bottoms and sides. Tacked to the back of one drawer you find an envelope, addressed:

To be sent to the police in the event of my sudden death.
John Symington

You show it to McDonald, and the Inspector smiles. "You read it," he says. "You found it." Almost shaking in your eagerness, you open the envelope, pull out a letter, and begin to read.

Metropolitan Police, Scotland Yard

Sirs,
As some of the less kindly of your officers have sug-
gested, I have operated my businesses in an illegal and
fraudulaet manner, designed to separate fools from their
money.
I neither boast of nor apologize for these activities. By
the time anyone reads this letter, I will be beyond the reach
of human judgment. My purpose in writing is to insure that
my partner in these endeavors does not escape the law. If I
die suddenly and violently, he will almost certainly have
murdered me. He has given me the money to finance my
initial operations, has referred investors to me, and has
taken a large percentage of the profits. His name is
Christopher Marshall, of London.

John Symington

You and McDonald exchange excited glances. *Check Clue S.*

- If you checked Deduction 21, **turn to 480.**
- If you checked Clue E or Deduction 8, **turn to 138.**
- Otherwise, **turn to 482.**

Perkins is positively eager to help you. First he shows you the regular files. There is not much there, but you do find a note that Sir Terrence repaid Marshall a loan of 3000 pounds on the last day of 1893. "Is this all?" you ask. "Were there any other records?" *Check Clue W.*

Perkins hesitates for a second, then manipulates the back of a cupboard and pulls out more papers. "These were the master's secret files," he explains. "Perhaps they will help."

You thank him again, and go through this new group of papers. Here you find direct evidence of the illegal operation of Sir Terrence's companies. Further examination turns up evidence that Marshall was his hidden partner in all these efforts. There is a note that Marshall loaned him 300 pounds to start a company on January 1, 1893. This was to be listed in the books as a 3000 pound advance. This permitted the false entries in the books to document the company's 'efforts' to find gold on the Ivory Coast. Actually, the company never did anything except take money from gullible investors. *Check Clue X.* **Turn to 501.**

582

You remember the little table lying on its side and you wonder if Lawrence noticed it. "There was one odd thing in the billiard room," you say to the captain, and he looks at you with an interested gleam in his eyes. "The little table by the armchair near the windows was knocked over sometime during the evening. Did you notice whether this had happened before you came into the room?"

Lawrence shakes his head. "I can't say that I did, sir, I was trying to watch the men rather than physical things. But with all the men who were milling around that room, I wouldn't be surprised if one of them bumped it without even noticing what he had done." **Turn to 116.**

583

Having given such attention to the room, you decide to look very carefully at the billiard table and the area around it. Though impatient with you, Strickland at least admits that this search makes some sense. **Pick a number** *and add your Observation bonus:*

- *If 2-7,* **turn to 241.**
- *If 8-12,* **turn to 420.**

584

The behaviour of the man going up to Symington's office is suspicious. You decide to follow him. You wait a few seconds to let him get past the landing, then you carefully open the door and enter the building. Moving silently, you hope that the visitor won't hear you. **Pick a number** *and add your Artifice bonus:*

- *If 2-7,* **turn to 220.**
- *If 8-12,* **turn to 309.**

585

"I am sorry that I wasted your time," you say quietly, "I feel certain that you have told me everything that you know. Thank you for your time."

"Think nothing of it sir," he answers sharply, and almost marches from the room.

Strickland glances at you, and you see a pleased look in his eyes. "You don't know quite everything, do you?" he says quietly. "Tact is very useful, especially when you are dealing with proud and sensitive men." **Turn to 380.**

586

"As you know, Captain," you begin, "I am investigating the death of Sir Terrence Milton, who was murdered last night. I would appreciate it very much if you would tell me what you thought of Sir Terrence; what kind of man was he?"

"Sir Terrence?" he answers, surprised. "His character doesn't matter any more, does it? He's dead. But I hardly knew the man; I couldn't tell you anything of use."

- *If you try to get him to say more,* **turn to 413.**
- *Otherwise,* **turn to 305.**

"A murderer?" the captain repeats. "So that's why he paid me to keep the boat waiting." He quickly turns the launch back to its dock, where McDonald and his men are waiting for the murderer. When you join them the Inspector congratulates you on your success. While the constables take Marshall to Cannon Row police station, you and McDonald take a hansom to Pall Mall and report to Mycroft Holmes. **Turn to 231.**

MIDDLE-EARTH ROLE PLAYING™

MIDDLE-EARTH ROLE PLAYING (MERP) is a Fantasy Role Playing Game system perfect for novices as well as experienced gamers! Based on THE HOBBIT and THE LORD OF THE RINGS, MERP provides the structure and framework for role playing in the greatest fantasy setting of all time....J.R.R. Tolkien's Middle-earth! MERP is well supported by a wide variety of game aids, Campaign Modules, Adventure Supplements, and Ready-to-Run Adventures. MIDDLE-EARTH ROLE PLAYING....a world apart!

Produced & Distributed by
IRON CROWN
ENTERPRISES INC.
P.O. Box 1605
Charlottesville, VA 22902

Rolemaster™

I.C.E.'s advanced Fantasy Role Playing Game system. ROLEMASTER is a complete set of the most advanced, realistic, and sophisticated rules available. The flexibility of the system allows it to be used wholly or in part. ROLEMASTER's component parts include: CHARACTER LAW & CAMPAIGN LAW, ARMS LAW & CLAW LAW, and SPELL LAW. Each of these can be used separately to improve the realism of most major FRP systems! Now you can add detail to your fantasy gaming without sacrificing playability! ROLEMASTER....a cut above the rest!

Produced & Distributed by
IRON CROWN
ENTERPRISES INC.
P.O. Box 1605
Charlottesville, VA 22902

Space Master™

Now you can adventure in space with I.C.E.'s
Science-Fiction Role Playing Game system!
Experience life aboard a deep space Outstation,
become embroiled in the constant conflict
between the ruling Houses of the Core
Provinces, or travel to the frontier in search of
vital resources. SPACE MASTER includes
guidelines for a wide range of technologies —
from tomorrow to the far future. Its rules cover
professions, races, cultures, settings, starship
construction, personal and vehicular combat,
and much more! SPACE MASTER....
the challenge of the future awaits!

Produced & Distributed by
IRON CROWN
ENTERPRISES INC.
P.O. Box 1605
Charlottesville, VA 22902

SHERLOCK HOLMES SOLO MYSTERIES

SHERLOCK HOLMES SOLO MYSTERIES present a series of living novels designed for solitary play. Each gamebook is an original mystery which the reader/detective must solve (with a bit of help from Holmes and Watson). Since the reader's choices affect his ability to unravel the mystery, SHERLOCK HOLMES SOLO MYSTERIES can be played again and again! So grab your magnifying glass and prepare to match wits with the master sleuth! SHERLOCK HOLMES SOLO MYSTERIES . . . . having fun was never so elementary!

Produced & Distributed by
IRON CROWN
ENTERPRISES INC.
P.O. Box 1605
Charlottesville, VA 22902

WE NEED YOUR FEEDBACK!

PLEASE HELP US DO A BETTER JOB ON FUTURE BOOKS BY ANSWERING SOME OR ALL OF THE FOLLOWING QUESTIONS & SENDING YOUR REPLIES TO I.C.E.:

I purchased this book at _____
_____(name of store).

The name of this book is _____
_____.

I am (male/female) _____, and _____ years of age. I am in the _____ grade in school.

I live in a (small, medium, large) _____ town/city.

My favorite magazine is _____.

I heard about this gamebook through_____
_____ (a friend, a family member, an advertisement, other _____).

The one thing I like the *most* about this Sherlock Holmes Solo Mystery is _____
_____
_____ .

The one thing I like the *least* about this Sherlock Holmes Solo Mystery is _____
_____
_____

Send all feedback replies to:

**IRON CROWN ENTERPRISES
P.O. BOX 1605, DEPT., SH
CHARLOTTESVILLE, VA. 22902**

RANDOM NUMBER TABLE

6	11	8	9	7	5	6	9	8	5	7	3
7	4	10	6	3	12	7	2	10	8	4	11
9	6	5	7	4	8	5	6	9	7	10	8
8	5	7	3	6	11	8	9	7	5	6	9
10	8	4	11	7	4	10	6	3	12	7	2
9	7	10	8	9	6	5	7	4	8	5	6
7	5	6	9	8	5	7	3	6	11	8	9
3	12	7	2	10	8	4	11	7	4	10	6
4	8	5	6	9	7	10	8	9	6	5	7
6	11	8	9	7	5	6	9	8	5	7	3
7	4	10	6	3	12	7	2	10	8	4	11
9	6	5	7	4	8	5	6	9	7	10	8
8	5	7	3	6	11	8	9	7	5	6	9
10	8	4	11	7	4	10	6	3	12	7	2
9	7	10	8	9	6	5	7	4	8	5	6